GUILTY NAMES

By Greg Currey

I

Mother had always been a widow, at least for as long as I had been alive. Father had died long before my birth and, if the conventions of science are to be believed, significantly before my conception, as well. I had never known a Mother without widowhood, without mourning, without a deep sorrow masked by solemn austerity.

At her best, Mother acknowledged and tolerated me. "You must listen to the priest and do as he says, and you will grow to be a good young man," she would tell me. I would respond with a nod, and if she were feeling particularly generous, she would say "it is not too late for you." For my eldest siblings, however, it was too late. "They are already corrupted by their own knowledge, already too sure in their own presumed brilliance," Mother once told me. Her eldest children Sirlat, Yhako, and Ansidrion were already lost to her, so I was to be nurtured in the image of her new philosophy, that I might avoid their fate.

"She had not always been so rigid," Yhako reminded me one afternoon. "There are two people contained within that woman."

"So you have said many times, but I do not believe it," I argued. "I have only ever known one Mother. You have invented the other to seem more like you, to justify your errant behavior."

"Oh, but there was another Mother, Federan. She was intelligent, thoughtful, and loving. She encouraged her children to question authority and seek their own answers. I wish you could have known her, rather than the ignorant, arbitrary, cold woman who forsook her eldest children and terrified her youngest."

"Then why have I never met this woman? If she was contained within Mother, she certainly should have made a few appearances."

"She lived in a different era. The first one was the enlightened Fulviya. But she disappeared shortly after Father's death, leaving you to be raised by the later one I refer to as Mother."

"How fortunate that she disappeared before I was born, so that I could never contest her existence," I said.

"It was the very circumstances of Father's death and your birth that led to the radical transformation," Yhako continued. "Thirteen months passed between these two events, and this impossible length of time exacted a terrible toll on Mother."

"Why should I value your recounting of her?" I demanded. "You have never loved Mother and I would not trust you to say an honest word in her memory."

"Federan, I would not criticize her so soon after her death. I did love Fulviya. I loved her for the first twelve years of my life."

I sat with my arms crossed and said nothing in response. I did not wish to hear Yhako's account, but I also wanted to learn more about Mother and her past, and I had no more reliable source.

"Mother had been a different woman entirely," Yhako went on. "She was among the few in the enlightened city of Ilepya to learn to read, as she had taught herself with scraps of letters and documents that she had, in her youth, scavenged from the alleys outside of aldermen's homes. She passed onto us a deep curiosity and admiration for letters, as she believed these carried all the secrets of science and of people's souls. It was Mother who, shortly before Father's sudden death, encouraged Sirlat to study at the University of Grontinion, where women are freely admitted."

"I do not believe it," I insisted. "Mother hated that place, and condemned it to me many times. This does not sound anything like the Mother I knew."

"She was not the Mother you knew," Yhako agreed. "It was merely the same body. Fulviya believed in learning, in the sciences, but when you appeared, those sciences were thoroughly discredited. It shook her very foundation. Nothing she had ever believed could explain why she had either carried a child in her womb for over a year, or conceived you four months after her husband's death."

"Then do you believe, as Ansidrion accused to me last week, that I am not Father's own?"

"Oh Federan, you must not take everything that Ansidrion says seriously. I know that your relationship is troubled now, and both of you say things with the intent to hurt one another. But I do not believe he meant what he said. I see plenty of Father in you."

I smiled—a rarity in those days, especially when I was with my brothers. "So how did she change? What was Mother's reaction?"

"She had just lost her husband and she was already seeking explanation of this from the world. So when this came along—when you came along—she cast aside everything that she had ever known. The only place that offered her any answers was the church and the Order which dictates the events of the universe, so she transformed in an instant to a woman who believed in the church's teachings completely, and cared for nothing outside of what it offered."

I did not like Yhako criticizing Mother as a woman alienated from logic, and I was feeling defensive about her memory, so I cut back at him. "Most people would praise her for seeking answers in the Order when she had nowhere else to go. And yet you treat it as a foolish mistake. What else was she to do?"

"She could have left us here in Ilepya, as a start. Instead, she dragged us to Kapabaj, that miserable country village in which no one was corrupted by learning," Yhako said, a touch of sarcasm to his description. "If she needed answers from the priests, she might have done so in moderation. Instead, she intended to correct Ansidrion and me, to clear our heads of all the great knowledge we had accumulated so far. But we were too old at that time, and as we already knew better, she had no way of changing our beliefs. So she turned her attention to our sister Qhema, and especially you, whom she could mold from birth."

"And I am glad that she did, for I would rather live my life at peace with the world around me, following the Order, than constantly question those who know better, as you always do."

"Federan, there is no peace in merely acceding to the world. What use are we if do not ensure the world's improvement by questioning it?"

"You make no improvement of it, but rather seek to destroy it. I have had enough of your nonsense for the day," I said, and stormed off and into my bedroom.

But my great struggle with my brothers will come later, for in my infancy and childhood, I had few interactions with them at all. They spent much of their days in their studies, although when they could bother a thought for me, they would call me *dofit*, or boy, and treat me with the condescended affection that was suitable for two grown men to don with a child. No, with a mother governed by severity, one brother who was the living embodiment of sloth and vain pursuits, and another who was far too brilliant and visioned to be trusted, it was Qhema who supplied me with my desired affection.

My sister was a decade older than me, and I was only about six years of age when she left, but in her boundless warmth, she left an indelible mark upon me.

She spoke to me with patience, and cared for me when Mother lost hers. When Mother would scold me for asking questions, or when my eyes would well with tears after Yhako failed to notice me outside of his study, Qhema would appear as if from nowhere, lift me up in her arms, and tell me one of the tales that Father had imparted to her many years before.

What I loved most—and remembered best—about my sister was how she made music with her voice. There was not much music to be heard in the house. Singing was too cheerful for Mother, while serious young men like Yhako and Ansidrion could not be bothered with the arts. But I cannot remember a night from my infancy when Qhema did not sing me to sleep. I learned, many years later, that she did not have much of a talent for it, but her sweet, melodic whispers comforted my lonely childhood. There was nothing that cheered me so much as the sound of her voice, the strength of her arms, and the light of her smile.

I became convinced, especially after she left, that Qhema was not my sister, but a delegate of the Order, who had come to attend to me with love when the others around me could not provide it. Once, when I was nine years of age, I obstinately argued to Ansidrion that he had never seen or known Qhema, and that she had been visible only to me. "If you believe you knew her, it is only because I have spoken of her many times to you, and she has come to seem a real person in your memory," I insisted. There was, of course, a mountain of evidence to the contrary, but my nostalgia for her, spurred forth by the coldness of life without her, encouraged me to deny anyone else access to her memory.

* * * *

Qhema and my brothers must have enjoyed nothing about Kapabaj. Nothing of interest happened in the village streets, and most of the people living there had time for little other than their labors. The boys were given into the care of the local priest, Dalho, who only had a flock of perhaps six hundred other people to care for.

"He was not much of a priest," Yhako told me several years later.

"Dalho was not much of anything," Ansidrion interjected.

I did not welcome Ansidrion's intrusion, but I did not say as much.

"Mother gave us to him, but he did not have much interest in teaching us anything," Yhako went on. "We wanted to learn, as Father had taught us. But the priest could not even read. Indeed, I do not believe that there was a single book in Kapabaj that was not in our house."

"Then why did Mother submit us to him?" I asked.

"Because he was the only priest in town," Ansidrion said. "And because Mother had plenty of money, which she misused following Father's death. She was easily the wealthiest woman in Kapabaj, and she could afford to make Dalho the wealthiest man."

"Yes, with a little financing of his lifestyle, Mother found that Dalho would gladly give up all but a few of his most important responsibilities in order to serve our family as she demanded," Yhako said. "And so, as her pregnancy continued on in its seemingly interminable progress—and it neared a year when she brought us to Kapabaj—Dalho took charge of us, becoming essentially a servant unto her."

"I cannot think of anything more proper than to live under the guidance of your priest," I said, knowing they would heartily disagree. I was thirteen then—old enough to put up an argument against them, but still without the capability to ensure it was a good argument.

"Do not mistake us for willing pupils," Ansidrion said. "Dalho was not intellectually equipped for the task of educating men such as us."

"I spent very little time in his presence," Yhako admitted. "I preferred the garden, where I could read and write outside of his watch."

"I could not be bothered to escape that far!" Ansidrion seemed to boast.

"I remember the time Mother found those translated documents of yours, Ansidrion," I said. "What were they?"

He glared at me. "We shall not speak of those!"

"But I recall them well." Indeed, I could remember Mother dragging me into a room where an uncomfortable Ansidrion stood waiting.

"Your brother has done a terrible thing, Federan," Mother cried. "He has defied me!" She struck his face and he recoiled. "He has defied the priest!" She said, slapping him once again.

I began to cry. I was but five years old at the time, and although I had not been particularly close with Ansidrion, I had never seen something like this. "Please stop, Mother!" I whimpered. "What has he done?"

"This!" She shouted, scooping several documents up from a nearby table. "He has read letters and essays that are strictly forbidden. They encourage corrupted men like your brother to question the prophets and everything underneath. They make this house unsafe for us!" Almost all in one motion, Mother threw the documents into the fire, shoved Ansidrion to the ground, and jumped on top of him. I sobbed and wailed for Mother to stop. She hollered and screamed at Ansidrion, pounding upon his body. Only Ansidrion was silent, as he drew himself into a ball and bore Mother's fists.

I cannot say how long this went on, but when Mother had finally tired of it, she shrieked and ran from the room. Ansidrion remained on the floor, unmoved, although at length, he glanced up and barked at me to leave his presence. He was a large, healthy young man, and Mother had already begun to weaken from the lack of care she gave her body, so I do not believe he was injured physically. Instead, he was humiliated by the experience. He concealed himself from me for the next week, and then, abruptly, he and Yhako fled the house for the city of Ilepya. They were stocky young men of seventeen and eighteen years by then, and it had come time that they take on the family *as'shelik*, or silk, business.

"There is little for our brothers in Kapabaj," Qhema explained to me. "I am surprised they had not left for Ilepya long ago."

"But what can be there for them?" I asked.

She shook her head. "I cannot remember, exactly. I was but a child when we left. But in my mind as I reimagine it, Ilepya was a great, bustling city, with halting contrasts and beautiful coincidences."

"That sounds frightening," I admitted. "There is too much complication, and I have no wish for any of that."

She had been looking off, into a distance which I was as yet incapable of perceiving. When my small voice called her back to attention, she looked at me and sighed. "Poor Federan. You have never known any other life. But perhaps you will someday. There is a thirst, a curiosity for it in every member of the Ponyhubiresh family." And then she pulled me into her lap and I fell into a sleep where there was neither Ilepya nor Kapabaj, Ansidrion nor Yhako, but only Qhema's peaceful music.

Qhema, herself, left shortly after. "At her request, I have sent her to a distant land to minister to the Vendi people," Dalho explained. "She will teach the ignorant about the prophets and the Order."

I discovered a note next to my bed, and I recognized her signature upon it. Yet I could not make any sense of any of the letters, so I brought it to Mother. "I miss Qhema very much, and will only come to long for her more in time," I began with all the courage I had. "Please, tell me the content of this message."

But Mother refused to take the paper into her hand. "I shall not," she said.

I did not beg, and Mother was not one to be begged.

"You should not obsess over those who have left," Mother scolded me. "All of those who enter your life will leave it. There is nothing for you to do but to forget about them as they have abandoned you."

I was devastated when Qhema left, but I did not miss Yhako or Ansidrion, nor did I despise living alone with Mother. This life with Mother and Dalho in Kapabaj was all I had ever known, and I did not want for much aside from the affection with which Qhema had supplied me. My brothers had begun teaching me how to read, but they never gave much time to it, and I learned very little. Mother did not value literacy, so she directed all of my learning to memorizing prayers and understanding church hierarchy. First, above all else, I was to follow the word of the priests and the Iqharepur, the head prophet of our church, who lived a thousand miles away.

As much as possible, Mother kept to herself and encouraged me to keep to myself. "Only terrible things can come of speaking out, of making the world take notice of you. You will be attacked and ripped down. Instead, you must always be quiet, and you must always listen and do as you are told." Like the son she wanted, I never questioned or even responded to these instructions.

They continued to inform my actions even when I was old enough to know better.

Ansidrion did return for occasional visits, and during those days he spent much of his time with me. He taught me a few games and attempted to improve my education, but his presence was too infrequent to have much of an effect. Yhako never visited, although he did write occasional letters. These, of course, went directly to Mother, who would merely tell me "Yhako has asked your fare and wishes you well."

Dalho died when I was ten, and was replaced with a priest from the town of Pondital. The new priest brought with him modest wealth, and thus Mother found him difficult to control. She no longer had the energy or desire to look after me, and the priest was unwilling, so for a few months, I lived independently, left to my own devices without lessons or orders. Then, perhaps as a remedy to this, we picked up suddenly and returned to Ilepya, that den of filth and heresy that Mother had abandoned a dozen years ago.

Initially, I liked living in Ilepya. I missed Kapabaj, as it was all I had ever known, but Ilepya was new and exciting. We made our residence in the family home with Yhako and Ansidrion, who surely were not happy at sharing a roof with Mother again. "You are never to speak with your brothers," Mother had instructed me when we first arrived. But she did not have the attention or will to enforce this rule, and Yhako and Ansidrion appeared interested in me anew. So, for the first several evenings, while Mother remained prostrate in prayer, they would come and begin teaching me to read as they had years ago.

Some days, my brothers would bring me to Maidia Square, the city's central plaza. I had nothing but a happy view of those occasions. My brothers were successful merchants by then, and they would call me *dofit* and I would feel proud when they would nod to important men and women that they knew. Ilepya was full of exciting things, and in one day I might see more people than lived in all of Kapabaj.

It was in those first days in Ilepya that I began to learn details about Father and what the Ponyhubiresh household was like before his death. "He was a man of great height and size," Yhako recounted, "much like the Ansidrion you see today." He motioned toward my heaving, mountainous brother, who nodded with a smile. "He valued knowledge and honesty above all things, and became a man of generous reputation throughout Ilepya."

"He grew to be a great collector of books," Ansidrion continued. "And although you might expect a premier merchant to build a grand home with many rooms, and keep several servants in his employ, Father was merely satisfied with the modest home in which we live today. He devoted his wealth to the accumulation of knowledge, which he considered the most potent of all riches. This is manifested in the library in our home. *Dofit*, the most valuable treasures in the world are in that library, and you will one day learn to partake in all of them."

Ilepya seemed so full of potential, so full of hope. I felt, for the first time since I had watched Ansidrion endure that attack by the fists of my mother, that I was capable of doing great things. Those shapes and lines I had seen all over letters and documents had meaning to them and, for the first time, I believed that I might learn to decipher that meaning beyond a few words. The world was open, and although those conversations along Maidia Street were in the midst of a cold, wet spring, I felt enshrouded by a serene light, which nurtured me and allowed my confidence to grow.

"Father was a great merchant of *as'shelik*," Yhako explained. "His wares were distributed throughout Hihaythea and all remote parts of the Great North."

"You trade in the *as'shelik*, do you not?" I asked.

"I do. Father instructed me, and I shall one day teach you, and so the skills and the trade will remain in the family."

"And Ansidrion?" I asked.

"I know the trade, yes," Ansidrion confirmed. "But I leave that to Yhako, who is much better suited to it."

"Let each of us do most what we excel at most," Yhako proclaimed. "I manage the business for both of us, and Ansidrion sleeps for both of us."

"He sleeps for both of you?"

"Yes. I sleep a few extra hours each morning and evening—enough rest for Yhako beyond the sleep I enjoy during the night. That way, Yhako has time enough to do all of the things he enjoys."

I yawned. "Might you sleep for me, as well? It is late and I grow tired."

"The sun has fallen, and it is time for us to return home," Yhako confirmed. We turned south and began walking along the same path we had come, as the people around us did likewise. "I am afraid Ansidrion has no hours to spare at present, but one day when you are older, you can spend the days studying with us, and use your nights for whatever pursuit you thrive at."

The city's marvels had continued to multiply by the day. "There are ten active priests in Ilepya, and I shall bring you to see one," Mother informed me the following morning.

"Why would you ever leave such a marvelous place?" I asked, astonished.

"There will be no more outbursts," she said, glaring at me.

I resumed my trained silence.

"He will not be like Dalho," she continued. "He will not see you every day. But he knows much more than that old fool."

She brought me to the old temple—a small, ornate marble building on Eparam Street—and led me inside. "You will listen faithfully and follow as he instructs in all things," she ordered. I nodded, and then she left me to fend for myself with him.

I was a shy young man, having been sheltered from strangers and much of the world. I went to see the priest with an immense curiosity, but merely setting my eyes upon him filled me with unease. I did not know how to speak with him, and I found his appearance unnerving. He had a terrible, jagged smile for a mouth, and his eyes were light and strange. His old nose hooked sharply downward, with bundles of hairs peering out from within the nostrils. He sat in a heavy wooden throne that looked fit for a great bishop, and as he spoke, he carefully traced the pointed spire atop his cane. I feared no evil from him, but I was disappointed at his wrinkled, weathered appearance, for I had hoped to meet a man who might be a bit closer to my age and provide better companionship.

"Hello, boy," he said softly as he smiled. He had a deep, graveled voice—the sort I would have imagined for an old bear—and his words came in huffs and grunts, emphasizing more sounds than practical. "My name is Masbat, but you may call me Ma't."

I nodded slightly, but was still too shy and fearful to say anything.

"Come, be seated." He motioned slowly at the small stool across from him. I noticed that he had the slightest of accents. I had never met anyone with affected speech, for there were no foreigners in Kapabaj, so I strained to record the new curiosities of the tongue. I took seven small, careful steps, never taking my eyes off of the priest, and lowered myself into the stool.

"Your mother tells me that your name is Federan, is that correct?"

I could not muster any words for him. I might have been shaking in fear.

"You are Federan, are you not? Can you speak?"

Finally, I managed to say "Fe'n," with a nod.

"Fe'n! So you shorten your name just as I do!"

"Yes, sir."

"That is good. You are a promising young boy already. I think we shall agree with each other just fine. And do I hear that you have two older brothers?"

"I do, sir."

"And yet, for all my time in Ilepya, I have never met either of them! Now why do you believe that is?"

I shrugged.

"I shall tell you why: because your brothers believe they know everything. Your mother has told me. They question others, yet are impossibly sure of their own knowledge. Can you imagine a life in which even as such a young man, you could not be convinced of anything other than what you already knew?" I gave no response so Ma't continued. "I am glad you are not like your brothers. I am glad your mother has reared you well. It is good that you have come to me to learn. You must be careful of the words that your brothers say."

He echoed what Mother had always told me. I had been wary of or disinterested in Yhako and Ansidrion, but the brief few days with them in Ilepya had suggested that they were not so terrible. But if my mother, and the Order and its prophets, were so critical of them, perhaps they might not be as pleasant as they seemed.

Ma't finished with more encouragements to follow the words of my mother and him, and then I found my own way home. The following evening, I accompanied my brothers once again to Maidia Square, and they began to speak and preach to me, as had become their custom. Yhako had been in the midst of telling some story about our sister Sirlat. The exact content of the tale I do not recall; I was too preoccupied attempting to muster the courage to question them about what Ma't had said. Besides, everything they had taught me about Sirlat in the last week would be, in an instant, shattered, such that I no longer valued or trusted a word of it. Those happy times in Maidia Square, and everything that I associated with them, were about to come crashing down as a direct result of the conversation I was to initiate.

"Why do neither of you see the priest, Ma't?" I asked abruptly, interrupting Yhako's story.

Both men looked at me and frowned. "The priest?" Ansidrion asked, sounding incredulous. But then, suddenly, he laughed. "I have no interest in that old man. He does not have any good idea about the ways of the world!"

"But Ansidrion, he is our minister appointed by the holy prophet, the Iqharepur. Of course he knows about the world. He is our only source of information on the Order!"

"You must not believe everything that Mother tells you," Yhako said, shaking his head.

Mother? What did this have to do with Mother? "But who should I trust if not my mother and my priest? Do you already think you are so wise that you have nothing to learn about the Order?"

"Nothing to learn about the Order!" Ansidrion scoffed. "We have said no word about the Order! That priest knows nothing about the world or the Order that governs it. All he cares is that the people come to him and receive instruction to obey his wishes. Ha, no, there be no prophecy, no sign of the Order in that temple."

How had they become such haughty men? "Mother and Ma't are right about you, then. You trust nothing so much as your own knowledge. You will not suffer any questions of what you know, for you believe that you are infallible."

"No, it is that priest and Mother who pretend they are infallible, for they will not accept any question or challenge to their word," Yhako said. "You cannot believe that they are the ones whose minds are more open, can you, Federan?"

I was fuming now. I had not intended to turn on them so rapidly, but they were just as arrogant as Ma't had said. "Fe'n. My name is Fe'n. Who are you to admonish me? You do not even know how to call me! Where were you in my youth when I lacked a father?" I felt strange and uneasy, but it was too late to contain my anger. I turned to Ansidrion. "You only appeared enough to teach me things that earned my mother's shame, and you," I said, looking at a stunned Yhako, "could not even be bothered to visit at all! You two claimed to value letters and studies so much, yet never ensured that your own brother could even read."

Before they had a chance to respond, I marched abruptly home. "I would like to train to become a priest like Ma't," I informed Mother as soon as the sun rose the following morning. "I shall learn to read and write, and make sense of Portavan, the language of the prophets."

Mother agreed to enroll me in a local grammar school, likely relieved to have somewhere else to store me during the day. I also continued to visit Ma't every week, and at our second visit, we discussed this new commitment.

"Your mother has explained to me that you aspire toward the priesthood," he began. "This is very good! I am glad to hear it. What has inspired you to this end?"

"I do not wish to be like my brothers. They are insufferable men, and have rejected Mother and you. That will not be how I am. I wish to learn from you, and to learn to lead people properly."

"Your mother has already planted the seeds for you, by raising you in accordance with the Order. Your birth was a miracle, as it set a wayward woman along the correct path, which ensured the same for you. Your presence in this very room, an offspring of the stray Ponyhubiresh flock, is a direct result of your wondrous conception! Perhaps that miracle shall continue to manifest itself, through you setting your brothers right."

"Oh, that is what I want most in the world!" I cried, the words leaping from my mouth before I had a chance to understand them. When I had first come to Ilepya, not even a month earlier, I had been excited and proud of my budding relationship with Yhako and Ansidrion. But suddenly we had broken, and now my resentment toward their ways, and their rejection of everything I loved, was rapidly dividing us. "I want nothing more than to become a priest of great learning, so that I may be wiser than my brothers and put a stop to their heresy, to their rejection of the Order!"

"There we are, my boy!" Ma't reached forward and patted my knee heavily. "There is some excitement and passion in you. You are already wiser than your brothers, for you have had the wisdom and courage to come here in search of truth, rather than giving in to their evil temptation. You tell those young men to pay me a visit if they are so brave and wise, and I shall set them anew!"

I smiled, at once at ease with this old man. He had attacked the men that I despised most of all, and it had won me immediately. Following that meeting, I found my way home and considered challenging Yhako and Ansidrion, as Ma't had suggested. But instead, I chose to bide my time, saving up my knowledge and fortitude until I knew I had enough to defeat them. I imagined myself in outright intellectual warfare, although I chose to avoid the pitched battle of true debate, instead winning skirmishes by turning my back on them and rejecting or denying whatever ideas they tried to press upon me.

With Mother's encouragement, I continued to visit Ma't, allowing him to fill my brain with thoughts and ideas that Sirlat and Yhako and Ansidrion hated, and that Mother reverently feared. I enjoyed coming to Ma't because he told me exactly what I wanted to hear, and affirmed me in every disagreement I had had with my brothers. One day, about three years after I had first come to Ilepya, I made the mistake of standing up to Yhako before I had sufficiently fortified my knowledge. He had caught me just as he began his studies in the evening, and as I prepared for bed.

"Do you still go on about the priesthood, *dofit?*"

I had saved my breath and bidden my time so long by that moment, so I decided that I was sturdy and studied enough to respond. "About and ever toward," I answered confidently. "How might a man do well in the world and advance the Order else he gives his life in devotion?"

"A better education would be a logical path," Yhako suggested.

"This is precisely how I spend my days, for Ma't teaches me about prophecy and the Order. But this is also where I fault you, for you believe education is the key to everything. You believe a person cannot succeed without reading and writing. So your beliefs can only be achieved and understood by those who have those luxuries. Yet mine are universal, for they belong to the literate and illiterate alike."

"Your beliefs seem universal to you because they are enforced on the population, and because you have constant access to a man who ministers them. Your church is not the path to understanding the way of the universe, but rather the State's means to controlling the people."

"This makes it no less universal. Every time I go to the temple, Ma't welcomes me. If I can visit my priest, what stops any other person from visiting him?"

Adopting the stale air of smugness, he stroked his chin. "Money, for one thing. You have unlimited access to your priest because Mother has bribed him."

I did not know this, and it made me uncomfortable. Still I pressed forward. "Ma't must make his living just as anyone else. How can he feed himself if not by accepting money offered from generous people?"

"So the poor do not deserve access? Does the Order not care for them? Is seeking the good will of the universe merely for the rich?"

I did not have an answer. No, everyone should have access, but I did not know how to rectify the problem. How could we achieve universality if access required payment? In response I merely grunted and retreated toward my chamber.

I was surprised along the way to encounter Mother, standing in the doorway to her bedroom. She was pale, with her cheekbones especially pronounced. Although her body swayed forth and back and her arms trembled at her sides, her eyes were wide, and looked into me without deviation. With the subtlest nod, she backed deliberately into her room and sat on the floor.

In the last several weeks, all I had known of Mother was the muted hum of miserable prayers that could be heard from outside of her door. I could not remember the last time I had seen her. I might not have had a single conversation with her since she had delivered me to Ma't and the temple, now three years before.

Following her silent orders, I stepped into the doorway and found myself looking down upon her. I remained motionless there, unsure of the intentions of the terrifying, woeful woman before me. "Enter, Fe'n," she instructed. Her voice was strong and direct—much more like her unrelenting stare than her withered, failing body.

I shuffled into the room, closed the door, and sat directly across from her. My head opposed hers, although it would be improper to say that we faced one another, for my face was pointed down at my hands in my lap. The floor was unforgiving, instilling pain into the forgotten bones of my legs.

"Do you mind your brothers?" She asked.

I looked up at her and frowned, before returning my gaze downward. "No, Mother. I follow the instructions of you and Ma't alone, just as you have said."

A period of silence ensued that seemed interminable. Finally, I took a breath to speak further, although I did not know what I intended to say. But Mother interrupted before the first sound emerged from my mouth. "You must do as your brothers tell you," she ordered.

"But Mother, they give me orders that are contrary to yours. They forsake you, they condemn Ma't. How can I obey all of you at once?"

"The world is a gravely dangerous place, full of loss, sorrow, and isolation. Your brothers are foolish young men. They are clueless to the perils of our lives, although I have tried on many occasions to correct them. They do not understand the risks they take, and will meet certain doom because of those risks. You must never be seen to follow Yhako and Ansidrion, but even so, I command you to honor and respect them in private."

"But I should continue to do as Ma't instructs? I should not allow Yhako or Ansidrion to interfere with this?"

Mother sighed deep and unevenly. Her chest quivered and she let out a whimper. "Yes. You should never cross the priest."

I nodded. I suspected that Mother had dropped her stare by now, but I did not yet dare look. Besides, I was far too confused by what she had instructed. She had never had praise—even as meager as this—for my brothers. And I could not reconcile the idea of honoring their instructions without being seen to do so, and while also doing exactly as Ma't told. At length, I whispered "thank you, Mother," and stood and crept toward the door.

"Give me your word." She demanded.

I leapt and looked over at her to find that her eyes were still locked on me. I nodded vigorously.

"Your word, Fe'n."

"Yes, Mother. I shall honor Yhako and Ansidrion, while doing as Ma't instructs."

"And Sirlat."

My eyes widened, but I quickly suppressed my surprise and hesitation. "I shall honor Sirlat, as well," I agreed.

Now she lay down again and began to wail her prayers, so I hastened out of the room, shutting the door behind me. It was only once I had left that I realized how terribly the room had smelled. My thoughts and feelings blurred into one another, and I had no way to make any sense of what had just occurred. But the following morning, I was to be given an excuse to dismiss all of it outright.

Troubled by that conversation, I attempted to conjure Qhema's voice to comfort me to sleep, but I was frustrated of recalling any of her songs. Then, the following morning, Yhako discovered Mother's body, sprawled across her bedroom floor. "I had not heard her prayers in several days," he explained. "Finally, this morning, I entered to ensure that nothing was amiss. I am afraid she is already gone from this world." He wrapped his arms around me to muster as much warmth as he could.

I was not particularly in need of comfort, as Mother had never been a great source of love or guidance for me. She had been in poor health for most of my life, and had neglected me for the past several years. The only remaining thing I needed from Mother was further explanation as to her last instruction. But perhaps they had only been part of her final delusions. Yes, they made no sense to me because they were illogical. Mother had been so close to death at that point that she was beyond worldly sense, and thus, her last dictate could be ignored.

Mother's will entrusted my care to Ma't, but I believe this came as a surprise to even him. In truth, Yhako and Ansidrion would be much more active in my daily life. They saw to my basic needs, and tirelessly devoted themselves to changing my beliefs, although I refused to be moved.

Despite our constant conflict, my brothers attempted some comfort toward me: Yhako took time from his day to show me a few accounting strategies he used, while Ansidrion introduced me to a few of the foods that he most enjoyed. They did not fulfill my every wish, however. A week after Mother's death, they revoked my tuition at the grammar school. "It is an institution of the corrupt state and church," Yhako insisted. "It teaches nothing more than that you be complicit in and supportive of their theft, so you will no longer attend that place."

"But what about my literacy? How would you, who claim to support education, keep your own brother from learning?"

"You have gone there for three years yet you cannot even read!" Ansidrion said. "Our money shall not go to them, Federan."

"We shall find another, more appropriate school for you to attend," Yhako decided. "You will learn to read, but not at a place that teaches you to blindly follow the Iqharepur. A few of our friends have opened a small, secret school that follows the ways of the reform, the *deshilva*, and you can begin there two days hence."

"I shall not set foot in a *deshilva* school!" I cried. "You will have to drag me there by my ears!"

"Very well, that we shall," Yhako agreed calmly.

Accordingly, on the designated morning, I remained in bed, hoping to avoid my brothers entirely. I knew it was futile, but if they would make me go to a reformist school, I would at least make it as unpleasant an experience for them as it would be for me.

About a half hour after sunrise, Ansidrion lumbered into my room. "You have missed breakfast, and so will go hungry at school today," he grumbled. "Tomorrow you will learn to wake up earlier." I said nothing and remained still, so my brother barreled toward my bed and spoke again. "Now let you rise, for the sooner we get you to school, the sooner I can get to my own studies." Still, I offered no response. "Come, Federan, you have desired nothing more than to learn to read and write. This school will be your means to that." Silence. "Very well, as you will," he growled, stomping out of the room.

Then there was nothing. Had I won? No, it could not have been so easy. Perhaps Ansidrion had gone to collect Yhako, who would find some way to trick me into going.

Some three minutes passed as I waited for Yhako's calm, sneaking voice. Instead, I heard the lumbering again. Why had Ansidrion returned? What would he try now? I rolled onto my side, such that I faced the door, and watched as he entered. "If you will not go on your own, I shall bring you there," he said through his teeth. He approached me with a raw aggression that I had never seen in him. My brothers had never used force against me. Would they now? Would Ansidrion take to me as Mother had taken to him? But he was a hulking giant; probably three times my size! I had never thought to fear my own safety from him, but he was quick to anger, and perhaps he was capable of it now that Mother was no longer around to prevent him.

I shut my eyes tightly as he approached. He grabbed me by the wrists and I allowed him as he would, knowing that I could not beat his strength. He held my hands together in one of his hands, and then I felt him wrap a rope around my wrists. He released his grip, but now the rope bound me. Then, he lifted me into the air and carried me down the stairs. I opened my eyes to see Yhako watch with approval, as Ansidrion placed me into an iron cart. Had I suddenly become a prisoner of my own brothers?

"Do not be too long, Ansidrion," Yhako called as Ansidrion wheeled me out the door. "We shall need that cart for deliveries later."

Perhaps they had intended me shame by this, but I felt none. They were the dishonored men, the high and great scholars and merchants, reduced to carting their brother through city streets. I had the blessing of anonymity. It was Ansidrion who should have felt shame, for even in a place like Ilepya, of daily new and strange happenings, his actions brought stares and frowns.

"We shall do this every day if we must," Ansidrion leaned down and whispered into my ear. "And the more it happens, the worse it will be." But I felt my resolve grow strong, as I knew exactly what I had to do.

He delivered me to a small, inconspicuous building, inside of which a few dozen children were practicing their reading. I was placed to study with a dozen pupils well below my age, but I had no intention of absorbing any information. The master provided us with a book to which I gave no attention. "Do not allow anyone to tell the Bishop what you have read here," he said, "for he will not suffer any education against what he enforces." I scoffed in response, but gave no pause to the master, as he continued by having a few boys read the text aloud before the group.

The students droned in succession about the alleged misdeeds of the Bishop and our priests. "He has abused the liberties of the people," one recited.

"He has oppressed us all," another read.

I heard nothing but criticism of the Bishop and prophets in the book, just like the drivel my brothers had forced upon me. How could such a school exist here? It preached heresy, treason! It had no business in this country.

When it came time for me to read, I said nothing. The master encouraged me forth several times, but I was impervious to his demands, and would not be moved. Finally, attributing it to shyness, he moved on.

I closed my mind, attempting to immunize myself against their inflammatory rhetoric. How could they turn even such young children against the church? Two hours into the day, I could tolerate no more of this. "I must relieve myself!" I shouted abruptly. I ran out of the door and into the street, making my way directly for the grammar school I had once attended. The master there turned me away, however, as I was now unpaid. I had nowhere to go; I could not return home until studies ended at the *deshilva* school, some five hours hence. I had not eaten yet and I had no coin on hand. Instinctively, I began walking to the temple to find Ma't.

The old priest was consorting with another young man, but he permitted me to wait in the chapel. As soon as he was available, he summoned me and made for a servant to bring me some bread. "What has brought you to me today, outside of the usual hour? Is it about your mother?"

I swallowed the hunk of bread I had stuffed into my mouth. "No, it is not. Well, I suppose it may be. Yhako and Ansidrion have forced me to a *deshilva* school this day, but I have escaped it. Know you of these schools' presence and content?"

"You have done well, Fe'n," Ma't said with a smile. "Yes, I know of these schools. Tell me, do you remember this institution's location?"

I had not paid much attention during my delivery. "I am not certain exactly. It was not very near to my house; perhaps it was closer to the sea."

"Ah, yes. I have heard of such a school in that neighborhood. Do you know what street it was on?"

"Hum." I thought for a moment. "Oh yes, I believe it was on Kalal Street."

"Good. You will not have to worry about that school much longer, my boy." He folded his hands in his lap and his eyes narrowed into a smile.

"But what of tomorrow, Ma't? They will surely send me there once again in the morning, and I cannot return, for I do not wish to hear any more of their foul ideas!"

"Of course you do not, for they are not worth consideration. Then you will do tomorrow exactly as you have done today, and escape as soon as you are able, and come here. This is a place for you, Fe'n, and though I might be otherwise occupied, you may come here as often as you need. But I shall tell of this school to the Bishop, and once he hears how it has corrupted your mind, he will not tolerate it any longer. Its end shall soon come, Fe'n."

The words of welcome contented me, for I had never felt that I belonged at any place in my life. But I also felt slight unease. "How 'its end?' What shall the Bishop do to the school?"

Ma't frowned, taken aback that I had even asked. "What shall he do? I do not know, Fe'n. I have never thought it was important in past incidents. I have merely reported inappropriate behavior to him, and he has taken such action that we might never hear of their heresy again."

"But have you never thought to ask him what he does?" It seemed strange to me to not want to know the final outcome of an action.

"No I have not. I do not wonder about things that are not my concern, Fe'n. I tell the bishop about the problem, and he finds a solution that is appropriate."

"But what if his solution is wrong? Would you not want to know that the action he takes is the correct one? Are you not curious?"

At this point, for the first time, Ma't's voice became stern with me. "No, Fe'n. I am not curious. And perhaps you should not be either." And then his tone lightened a bit. "You must learn to trust in those with more authority than you. After all, who might you know that is wiser than the Bishop? You surely do not think either you or I can question his actions."

"No, I do not. I did not mean to question the bishop. I suppose I simply wonder about too many things that should not interest me."

"You do, Fe'n. But you are learning, and that is most important. Now come, tomorrow when they send you off to the school, you will escape again and spend your day here. I shall not have the time to speak much with you, but you may pull aside a few books, and perhaps learn how to read a few words."

And so we built a routine; day after day, I feigned attendance at the *deshilva* school, but then stole away to the temple. Ansidrion continued to accompany me for the next few mornings, but I gave up resistance. The man was bound by sloth, and once he saw that I went willingly, he declined to accompany me for more than a block.

Some days, Ma't would counsel me, as he had during Mother's life. But on other days, when he was otherwise occupied, I would poke through his prayer books. I slowly taught myself how to read, using the foundation of what little I had learned in my infancy. I had a natural talent for it, and initially I felt content to be learning literacy as Mother had. I was finding books thanks to the charity of others, and using them to fill my mind with information. I found that I craved it, and this desire caused me to recognize letters and words at a remarkable pace. The more I learned, the faster I was able to learn. The more knowledge I discovered, the more I desired.

And then, one afternoon, I could not tolerate it any longer. I burst into Ma't's chamber and disrupted his meeting with an old man. "Ma't!" I began, before I could understand what I was doing. "Might I have some ink?"

Ma't gasped and frowned at me. His guest, wearing the blue shirt of the *asdesaj*, or police force, scolded me not to interrupt.

"I shall handle this," Ma't told the man. "Wait outside for me, if you will." The man stepped out of the door and Ma't responded to my inquiry. "Ink? You have no need for ink."

"But I do. I would like to begin writing."

"Writing?" Ma't asked, incredulous. "Fe'n, what is…you cannot write, nor do you have any reason to!"

"I believe I might be able to write. I have studied your books for many days, and my memory of the words I learned in my childhood has allowed me to understand more. Both our native Galmostan and doctrine Portavan I have come to comprehend, and would like to practice translating from one of these languages to the other."

"No!" Ma't shouted abruptly. Then, catching himself, he continued, "translation is something you must not undertake. Perhaps you should not have been reading to begin with. I should never have left you alone with those books. Fe'n, you must promise me that you will read no longer, for I had only intended that you recognize a few common letters."

I felt devastated. How could he wish to rescind my hard-won literacy? "But Ma't, what of the priesthood? I shall need to learn to read if I am to be a good priest."

"Literacy is hardly a requirement of the priesthood," he argued. "But I suppose if you are to lead men such as your brothers unto the truth, you should be able to read. Hum." He paused for a moment to mull this over. "Very well, then, it seems it is not something I can keep from you. But if you must read, you will not do so without direction, for there are many evil books in the world, and reading is a dangerous ability that exposes young men to corruption. No, you must only read under my tutelage, never taking a book into your hands without my permission."

This seemed quite a harsh order, and suspicious beyond that. But I had just seen—even if only for a brief moment—my freedom to read withdrawn entirely. Now that the liberty had returned, even under these strange and oppressive terms, I gladly accepted it. So, from that day forth, I spent most afternoons reading only the books from his shelf that Ma't permitted for me. He allowed me to write a few words on what I had read, but every afternoon before I went home, I spent about half of an hour discussing the contents of the books with the priest. "You should confer with me before you bring it to argument with your brothers. That way we can ensure you understand it correctly."

I agreed. After the universality question, I did not desire forming a debate against Yhako without Ma't's help. On most days I avoided my brothers entirely, but then one afternoon, I returned from the temple to find them in a state of distress. "Federan!" Ansidrion cried, the moment he saw me. "Federan, you are safe!" The two men rushed to me and folded me into their collective embrace.

I had never experienced such behavior from them, and indeed, after those days in Maidia Square, our positive interactions had come to a halt. "Of course I am safe," I scoffed, wriggling free from their arms. "Why have you doubted it?"

"The school on Kalal Street!" Ansidrion began. "One of our friends has come to us with the news that it had been shut down this morning. The teachers have been taken captive, with the children dispersed. We had not known what became of you, Federan."

My stomach sank, and I felt cold. My breath drew short. "I am safe," I managed, and then quickly began toward my chamber to avoid further questioning.

This effort was futile. "How have you escaped?" Yhako asked. "Where have you spent the afternoon hours?"

I began to walk faster, but my brothers pursued me. "Were you not at the school at all?" Ansidrion accused.

My feet stopped moving and my head fell. Then, sighing, I turned around to face them. "No I was not. I ran off the first day you brought me there, and have not returned since."

Ansidrion's eyes grew wide with anger. Yhako shook his head and glared at Ansidrion. "Did you not accompany him there every day?" But then, without waiting for an answer, Yhako turned to me. "If not at the school, where have you been spending your days?"

My voice fell to a whisper. "At the temple, with Ma't."

"Every day with that priest?" Ansidrion was full of rage, and I flinched from him. "Doing what?"

"Seeking his counsel. And I have used every other minute instructing myself to read."

"You have deceived me this threeweek? Every morning, you made as though to go merrily to the school, only as a means to fool your old brother?"

"Yes. I had not wanted to deceive you, but I could not continue to go to that school." Yet I thought little of this conversation at the moment. "But what about that place? Who has closed the school? What will they do with the captives?"

"I believe it was the *asdesaj*, on the will of the Bishop himself. As for the teachers, I do not know what shall become of them, but I would be surprised if they were ever seen again." Yhako seemed distressed, but not outright angry, as Ansidrion was. "It is a serious crime to preach a contrary doctrine, and I would imagine the Bishop will deal with them harshly."

"I had not wanted this," I said, shaking my head. "I do not believe what those people preached, but I also do not believe they deserved this fate."

"No, of course not," Yhako agreed. But I had not been trying to convince him. I knew that Ma't had brought this about, and thus I was the source of it. I did not like the outcome, but had Ma't not made a good argument? The Bishop was the man who made this happen, and I did not dare question his authority.

I certainly had many things to think about that evening, so I turned once again for my bedchamber. But Ansidrion would not allow me to get away so quickly. "Federan, we shall find you a new school. You will not escape virtuous learning."

I prepared to make a rebuttal, but Yhako stepped in first. "No. He cannot go back."

"Not go back?" Ansidrion shouted. "He must! He must learn about the reform!"

But Yhako held firm. "We have nearly lost him this time. We shall not submit him to this risk anymore."

I nodded at Yhako, and then disappeared into my bedroom. The following morning, true to their word, there was no talk of a new *deshilva* school. Yhako offered me bread and cheese, which I declined, and spoke with me in a pleasant tone. But Ansidrion took no interest in me whatsoever, only sighing pointedly as we ate.

I was not disturbed by Ansidrion's behavior. I had very little interest in either him or Yhako, although I responded to Yhako's cordiality with the politeness it deserved. But as soon as we had finished eating, my brothers retreated to the study, and I hastened to the old temple to speak with Ma't.

"Welcome and good morning!" The priest called to me, smiling as he always did.

I had many questions for Ma't that day, and none of them involved smiles. "Greeting," I began. "I have heard that the school on Kalal Street has been shuttered."

"Exactly as you have wished, my boy!"

"No!" I gasped. "I did not wish for this. I did not want the Kalal school to be raided!"

"But you have, Fe'n. You reported the school to me. You have done a good thing, and good has come of it."

"Closing the school was never my intention. I merely wanted to cease to attend it."

"And think of all the other young boys and girls who were forced to attend that school. They will cease to attend it, as well."

"I welcome that," I admitted. "But not at the cost provided. Yhako says that the instructors at the school have been taken captive by the *asdesaj*. They might be put to death, or kept in prisons for years."

"Is this not what they deserve? Think, Fe'n. These people have spread dissent; they have corrupted countless young minds. Death or captivity will prevent their evil from being further inflicted on our society."

"I would never wish death on them, no matter their crime. And eternal captivity merely for spreading ideas? It does not seem right to me."

"Well it need not seem right to you. If you do not agree with this outcome, then you must trust those who have arranged it. The Bishop knows more than either of us, Fe'n. If he has made this happen, we must abide by it without dissent."

I sighed and shook my head. "I suppose your words make sense, but once again, they do not sit well in my heart. If it pleases you, might I pass the day outdoors?" I was in no mood to spend any time around Ma't.

"Very well, perhaps a stroll might refresh you."

I left the temple and began walking with no charted destination. All of the ideas of the past days wrestled in my mind, and I had trouble making sense of them. The people did not deserve imprisonment. But how else could they be prevented from spreading lies? This walk did not help clear my mind; it only made everything seem more entangled. But I found that my body had led me toward Kalal Street. The building that had housed the *deshilva* school stood before me, and to my surprise, it seemed completely undisturbed. I walked past it and it was silent within, with no apparent sign of disruption. I turned around and walked by it again. The windows were boarded up, but they had been covered when the school was in session, as well. For all anyone could see, business within the building continued as it always had.

Perhaps nothing had happened at the school at all. Yhako and Ansidrion might have gotten the wrong news—it could have been a different school. Of course, I knew that this was false. The fact that there was no sign of struggle did not mean that there had been no struggle. But I wanted to believe that the school had been left in peace. It made everything else easier. So, as if to convince myself, I said aloud "everything is as it should be." Enjoying this phrase, I returned home, repeating it again and again in my head, preventing any ill from entering my mind.

I returned to Ma't the following day in a better mood, prepared anew to accept what he told me, and to follow his ways. It seems foolish now. I should not have gone back to him, but I loved the certainty that he offered me. Besides, to choose anything else meant to reject the beliefs by which I had been raised, which were the only things that truly mattered to me then.

Despite the strange instructions, the intervention in my access to knowledge, and the actions he took to shut down the school, Ma't was not all bad. I still trusted him above everyone else, and he had a way of convincing me I was enlightened. "You are a lucky young man, Fe'n," he would tell me. "Where your brothers have followed a path of ignorance, you alone have been spared, and led instead to knowledge." To the old priest I was a bright pupil, a beacon of hope among the people of Ilepya. "How many other young men seek such answers from their priest?" He asked me one afternoon.

Hum. I had not pondered it before. "In fact, how many, Ma't?"

"None but you! There are some people who come to me with regularity, but they are all older, and more troubled. You do have more questions than they, and are probably a bit more curious than is healthy, but you will only correct this with age."

I supposed I did ask questions frequently. I instructed myself at that moment to challenge less and accept more. Yet to my brothers, I accepted entirely too much. "You recite everything that man tells you, with never a thought to the contrary," Ansidrion had once scolded me.

Yhako was less harsh and, indeed, after the closure of the Kalal School, we continued to be cordial to one another. It would be an overstatement to say that we were loving; we rarely spoke and often quarreled. But our arguments seemed to be shadowed by a mutual respect. Where, during Mother's lifetime, he might once have said "Federan, that is false," since, he might instead say "now Federan, you know that is not so." This shift from sternness to gentle condescension might not seem like much, but it was evidence that he did not carry with him the sort of anger toward me that Ansidrion did.

Of course, Yhako also agreed that I believed too much of what Ma't said. One evening, when I was perhaps sixteen years of age, I returned home from the temple and confidently informed Yhako that his translation from Portavan into Galmostan without church supervision had alienated him from the Order.

"Come, Federan, do you truly believe such a thing?" Yhako asked, shaking his head.

"It is so. I have heard it this day from Ma't."

"You are an intelligent young man, and one day you will learn that few things that old man says are true." Perhaps Yhako had decided that this light-hearted yet unwavering disagreement was a better strategy for persuading me. He often grinned as he chided me. Certainly, his method was more effective than Ansidrion's blustery shouting.

"Yet I have instruction in this matter from my priest. What instruction do you have to the contrary?"

"I have reason. Think, Federan: if the Order did not intend for us to translate, why would we have brains capable of doing so? Indeed, why would the Order want us to do less than we were able, considering all that the Order had enabled us to do?"

"There are many things we are capable of doing, yet know very well we should not do, Yhako. You know that using our minds thus will lead us unto danger."

"Thinking has led many unto danger, but the far greater danger will have been to not think at all."

"I know that words such as these seek to corrupt young minds, and are the words that lead us ever astray from righteousness. Ma't has already said you will try to confuse me. He has said that you will put many words into my head that will muddy the right with the wrong."

"It is very like a man who is incorrect to claim that everyone around him lies. Yet if it is his intention to prevent you from knowing more, and thinking about more things, does that not tell you that his arguments are weak, and will fold when presented with evidence to the contrary?"

"And yet, exactly what you have just said is exactly what Ma't has warned to me. Thank you, Yhako, but I shall not think about the things you have said to me, for I know that they are not healthy." I smiled and shook my head at him, and then promptly retreated to my bed.

But the truth was, of course I thought about what Yhako said. I thought about everything he said. And I hated that I could not help but think about it, and yet it contradicted everything I believed. There was no way I could disprove any of it. Yhako was full of questions to which I had no answers. Yhako was full of challenges which I could not meet. I did not know how I could go on believing things that contradicted him, but I was determined. I wanted to follow Ma't because he was so full of answers. I loved that his beliefs were consistent. There was always certainty with Ma't. With Yhako there was never certainty; nothing was settled. He lived by it, but I could not tolerate it. Too much in my youth had been unreliable, such that certainty was the thing I desired most, and it was the thing that Yhako most denied of me.

Like on many other nights, I struggled to find sleep as questions of the day tormented me. Yhako's many complications crept into my mind, and no self-reassurance that everything was as it should be managed to silence them. I was old enough now for my solitude to bloom into a faint sense of despondency. There was no longer any comfort in the past, but the future seemed to hold so little. I thought of the priesthood, but by now it had become more of a planned escape than an aspiration. I attempted to will Qhema back to Ilepya, for her to lull me to sleep with her voice, but she ignored my silent pleas.

When I was around eighteen years of age, I fell into a new routine with Ma't and the temple on Eparam Street. Yhako instigated it. "You are an adult now," he noted. "Even if you do not study what we do, you should join us, at least for a few hours each morning."

"I have never shown any interest in studying with you," I retorted. "Why would I join you now?"

"Because we are your brothers. Because we love you, and would like to share our ideas with you."

"Yes, I know very well what your ideas are. You cannot spend a minute with me without attempting to change my mind about the world and the Order. You wish that I join you so that you may have even more time to corrupt me."

"Brotherhood is a mutual relationship, Federan!" Ansidrion admonished. "We have looked after you all of these years. Now you have obligations unto us."

"Will you not merely take breakfast with us every morning?" Yhako asked. "We might agree to speak only of things that we have in common."

I paused. I knew this to be some sort of trap, but I also knew that agreeing would compel Ansidrion to relent. "Very well, I shall agree to only this."

Ma't, for his part, objected to the idea, but not very heartily. He lacked the time needed to supervise me every minute of the day, so while he opposed my spending more time with my brothers, he had no means to prevent it. So we settled into this new way, in which I would consume breakfast alongside my brothers, generally remaining silent, and then spend a few afternoon hours at the temple, before returning home for dinner.

Every few months, letters arrived from our sister Sirlat, who was studying at the far away University of Grontinion. I had no desire to read the notes addressed to me, as I recognized Sirlat and the University to be sources of heresy and treason against what Ma't taught. I might once have been interested in the life of my eldest sibling, but she had spent so many words persuading me to change my beliefs, and so few words demonstrating any concern for me, that I no longer cared for what she had to say. Yhako and Ansidrion knew it, however, so they always forced me to sit while they read the letter aloud to me.

It was through the letters that Yhako found a way to break his promise. "Come, Federan, it is good for you to hear tidings from your sister."

"But she wants nothing other than to corrupt me, just as the two of you do."

"Sirlat loves you. She takes great interest in you. We report word of your progress to her, and she is proud of you."

"Proud of me? That woman stands for everything I hate! She cannot be proud of me. Do not force lies into my ears."

"Read the letter and you will see," Ansidrion growled.

I shook my head and took a great bite of fruit.

"Well if you will not read it, then I shall recount it to you." Yhako said.

"No, that is contrary to our agreement. You said we would never speak about things on which we disagreed."

"No, I said that we would only discuss what we had in common. And Sirlat is our sister—there is nothing more mutual to us than Sirlat!"

I grunted. I suppose they were correct in word, although not in spirit.

Ansidrion interpreted my lack of verbal response as agreement, and he began before Yhako had the chance. I did my best to ignore the words, but I did hear that our head prophet, the holy Iqharepur, had recently died. Not only were these words of consequences, but I also heard Yhako scoff at them. I thought this uncharacteristically disrespectful of Yhako, and I interrupted Ansidrion to say as much. "How can you scoff at another man's death?"

"I do not scoff at his death, but rather what I know to come next. Please, Ansidrion, continue."

"'The next Iqharepur is chosen through hereditary tradition, meaning that the office will likely fall to the six year-old nephew of the deceased."

Yhako and Ansidrion quickly looked to me, grinning in anticipation of my response. When I gave none, Yhako urged me on: "What do you think of that?"

"Very little." I shrugged. They always demanded to know what I thought of Sirlat's letters, as though to trap me in some sort of theological debate.

"Your Iqharepur is dead and you do not care who succeeds him? You see the Iqharepur as the man who predicts and understands the Order; how can you not be concerned about who is next selected for the position? See, Federan, how this system controls you? You accept that you should have no say over the very structures that run our lives. How can you not be critical of a system that says that power over millions of people should fall to a young boy, merely because he was the closest relative of the previous office holder?"

"Because this is not a decision for me to make, and thus I shall worry little on it. It is bound to have very little influence on my life."

"He is the leader of your church, is he not?" Ansidrion asked. "Very little influence on your life? What good is the church if its own leader will not touch your life?"

"The Iqharepur prophesizes the Order, and the Order does not change merely because one man has died. This is a decision to be made by the agency of others, and I shall leave me out of it."

"He brims with trust, Ansidrion," Yhako said. "He has such faith in his church structure that he accepts as its inalterable destiny that it will remain corrupt as it has ever been, and that he has no right or duty to participate in it. This fatalism is a bit too simple for a smart young man like you." He continued to face Ansidrion even as he was now addressing me. "Men are often put off their path by the glimmer of silver or the softness of silk."

"As the Order wills it, so it will be," I responded. Simple was not bad to me; what was simple was often best.

"Indeed, the Order has willed that Yhako and I turn our backs on this foolish old system, and we are happy with the Order for that!" Ansidrion said, his voice rising. "But let us continue with this letter. Let us hear Sirlat tell how they will replace that worthless, broken, accursed old man you called the Iqharepur."

"I shall hear no more," I responded, stifling the anger in my voice. "The appointment of the Iqharepur does not concern me, and thus I shall go to my room, where my studies will have more value." Before my brothers could protest, I slipped out the door. However, as I fed now on the foolish things they said, I only spent a few minutes away. I needed a moment apart from their voices to gather my thoughts and calm myself, but with this done, I stood a few feet off from the door to the parlor. My brothers were loud men, and I often had very little trouble hearing their voices from any part of the house. In this position, I could very clearly make out every word they spoke.

They had, by this time, moved on to a new subject. In her recent letters, Sirlat had been narrating to them the details of a revolution in Yafia, her country of residence. "The government is new in Yafia; the commoners are able to elect the people who govern their nation. It must be an exciting time to be in the city of Grontinion," Yhako had been saying.

"Indeed, the glorious news of this revolution is all Sirlat has been able to write of," Ansidrion agreed. "She appears to believe that revolution might even come to our beloved country of Hihaythea as it has now passed through our neighbors in Yafia and Colof. Are you as confident as she?"

"I am not. The Coels were driven to despair by their grasping monarch. The Yiffens are an uppity people, who were inspired by their university and their large middle class to take control of their nation. For the Hihaytheans there are no such powerful motives."

I heard someone sigh. I assume it was Ansidrion, as he was the man who spoke next. "I think as you do. When the Yiffens heard news of the revolution in Colof, they took up arms and wrought a new government for themselves. But what did we Hihaytheans do?"

"Nothing," Yhako agreed. "It was as though they did not even hear the cry for revolution."

"And now, as Grontinion and Yafia awaken from their years of slumber and discover all that is wrong with their old beliefs, Hihaythea remains in its deep sleep. All the other parts of the Great North—even Colof, where once backward peoples had lived—have turned toward progress. But now Hihaythea falls behind. We live under such tyranny, yet the people can imagine nothing better. I know not what might stir us from this complacency."

"I suppose I do not know, either. But something must."

This conversation seemed circular, lacking in logic to me. The Hihaythean people were so oppressed that we were content? Our lives were so horrible that we had no reason to turn against the government? It was as though opposites reigned in my brothers' minds. I was eager to hear Ma't's view of it; he would surely mock it to my delight. So I decided to pass by the temple and seek his word on it.

To my luck, Ma't was not occupied at the moment, so he welcomed me into his chamber with a "Fe'n, my boy! Let you come and be seated!" I positioned myself on the stool as usual. "What has brought you to me this fine morning?" The old man asked.

"I have quarreled with my brothers once again, although that is nothing new."

"No, of course not! It means to me that all is right with the world. Let you always seek to be in conflict with those two!"

"Yes, well this afternoon a letter has come from Sirlat, and they read it aloud to me. I care very little for what she has to say, but Yhako and Ansidrion continue to insist that I am ignorant merely for disagreeing with them."

"Ah, but that is always the way, my boy," the priest rasped. "Those who have spent their lives in pursuit of vain knowledge think themselves superior to all others. It is how they must be; if they do not diminish you for being unlike them, their pursuits will have become purposeless."

"That is so, for I hate the disdain with which they describe the Hihaythean people. I know that we Hihaytheans are good, noble people who follow the Iqharepur in all things. Yet to Yhako and Ansidrion, we are foolish creatures, poor, directionless souls."

Ma't frowned. "Tell me, my boy. What is it that they have said?"

So I recounted to Ma't the conversation I had overheard between my brothers about the need for a Hihaythean awakening. "How can they wish for a content people to realize their anger? If we are happy, why would they trouble this?"

"Your brothers are, indeed, quite foolish. The people do not need to be awoken from this slumber."

"That is exactly as I felt. We are content. Why do they insist that we must be asleep merely because we disagree with them?"

"The people do not need to be awoken to any such disagreement! They do not need to learn from your brothers; it is the role of the people to be humbly led."

"Led?" I asked.

"Yes, led. It is my task, under the Order, to direct the people away from wrong. Men like your brothers have interfered with this task, by complicating the public mind and sowing dissent. When uppity men like them offer so many choices, it is only natural that the people will drift down the wrong path."

"But why can the people not be given choices? If our way is the correct way—and I believe that it is— should most people not choose it if left to their own instincts?"

"Perhaps they should, Fe'n, but they will not. The common people are incapable of understanding the Order on their own. They must be guided to it, and there are too many corrupt men who are eager to deceive them away from our faith."

"Then to educate them should be enough. If the people can be so easily deceived, we should fill their minds with truth, so that there be no space for lies."

"Fe'n, you are a bright young man, and adhere to many pleasant ideals. But unfortunately, these ideals are not the way of the world. The only way we can protect people is to shield them from the errant alternative beliefs. Education is not the solution. Think of your mother, Fe'n. When she was the most educated woman in all of Ilepya, she was also the most misguided. It was only when she abandoned her worldly learning that she opened her mind to the proper way of the Order."

"Hum. I suppose you are correct on this matter." He had his facts correct, at least. And yet it felt wrong to me. How could the pursuit of learning lead a person to foolishness? If knowledge were bad, why should I come to Ma't with questions? But, as usual, I said nothing of this, nor did I act upon it. I continued to see Ma't just as much as I always did, because he was the only person who gave me the answers that I sought.

A month later, more letters from Sirlat arrived. These occasions always marked the peak of my interaction with Yhako and Ansidrion. I usually managed to avoid them, but when Sirlat's letters arrived, they chased me with vigor, and sought to fill my ears and thoughts with their puffed-up ignorance. This afternoon was no different. "I suppose you have not given many thoughts to Sirlat's words since she last wrote them to you?" Yhako asked me, the new letter in his hand.

GUILTY NAMES

There was some tension in the house, as just the day before, the *asdesaj* had apprehended one of Yhako's friends, on the accusation that he had written pamphlets against the Bishop. I did not know if it was true, nor did I want to know, for fear that I might be tempted to let word of it slip to Ma't and make the matter any worse. But, just as the threat to my life at the closure of the Kalal school had softened my brothers to me, so the disappearance of one of their friends softened me to them.

They did not have to pursue me very heartily anymore. I actually liked the challenges that they gave me; they were an opportunity to test my beliefs and resistance against their practiced rhetoric. I enjoyed clashing with the men whom Ma't had described as "prophets of heresy." Fighting them demonstrated the robustness of my faith. "No, Yhako, I have not. In fact, I have not even read a word she has written this decade."

"Today arrived a special note, Federan. Sirlat has explained it in her letter to me. She has issued you a challenge. Will you take it up?"

"I have no interest in Sirlat's challenges. Just like you, she is full of traps and tricks, and I know better than to subject myself to those."

"Will you not just read it? I believe it might help us find peace between one another."

"Peace by luring me to your side? No, I do not want this," I scoffed. But I was curious and, deep within me, I harbored a buried desire to live in harmony with my relatives. "But if you insist upon it, you may recount it to me."

"Very well, then. I shall." Yhako cleared his throat. "In his piece *The Miracles of the Order*, Maddith describes the Miracle of the Noble Laborer. Have you heard of the Noble Laborer?"

I shook my head.

"But you do acknowledge Maddith, do you not? And you recognize that his miracles are true and accurate?"

"Yes, I know that his work describes the miracles that help predict the way of the Order, and which may appear to those who are true of heart. Ma't has praised Maddith and I take his miracles as truth."

"Good. Now I shall tell you of Maddith's belief in the Noble Laborer. Maddith describes that belief in the Order is the natural way of things. He gives the example of the Lylyan people, who lived deep in the mountains and were not exposed to any outside influence for hundreds of years. They were a hearty people who, though intelligent enough, never learned to practice any faith. Then, suddenly, every belief system converged upon them, and they had to choose which they would adopt. And, because the Lylyans had remained in their natural state, and had never been exposed to any previous, undue influence, every last one of them chose to follow our belief in the Order."

"It sounds true, and I believe the word of it. But what is the challenge?"

"Patience, Federan. Maddith called these uncorrupted peoples the Noble Laborers. He predicted that, if ever this scenario could be replicated, the results would be identical. Of course, finding the next Noble Laborer has proven impossible; the remaining tribal peoples have either already been corrupted by one faith or another, or else are so hostile to all outsiders that they refuse to hear any religion at all."

"Then, while an important story that strengthens my faith, the Miracle of the Noble Laborer is irrelevant today, for it cannot happen again."

"Exactly as Maddith has described it, it cannot happen again," Yhako agreed. "But that is because Maddith died over three centuries ago. He passed before your church and your Iqharepur had reached the extent of their total corruption. Maddith did not foresee the current crisis, and therefore thought that the Miracle of the Noble Laborer was mere history as soon as he recorded it.

"But, in fact, the miracle has returned to prominence at the University of Grontinion. Yes, there remains no one who has not been exposed to any religion. But how many are there who are ignorant of the reform? Think, Federan: there are thousands of people who know nothing of what Sirlat, Ansidrion, and I believe. Think of all of the Noble Laborers who go about their daily business, believing in the Order and following the common laws imposed on them by their bishops, but giving nary a thought to prophets such as the Iqharepur, or the Lords' Occult? Perhaps you and I might find a Noble Laborer right here in Ilepya, and each argue our case to him. Do you think?"

I shrugged. "I suppose it is so. But how will we know if our subject has been corrupted or not? And who is to say you will not find someone and compromise him before you introduce him to me?"

"You and I can agree upon a test. Sirlat has recommended this challenge, and she says that you will recognize the Noble Laborer by his belief in the Order and his knowledge of a Midnight Ritual. Yet he will not be able to name the Seven Lords of the Occult, does not receive instruction from his priest but once a year, and does not know a single piece of religious literature by name. He should demonstrate that he is intelligent by being able to sign his own name and read a few basic words, but by virtue of his being a laborer, he will not be very concerned with letters, for these have little to do with his life."

"Very well. I accept your challenge." I knew I did not have a choice, because the challenge seemed so simple and honorable. If either side had an advantage, it was mine, because the Noble Laborer would have been surrounded his entire life by the priests and those who follow them. But the truth was that I did not want to take part in this. I hated the risk that something I so believed to be true might lose. And then what would I do? Besides, Yhako was sure to find a way to outsmart me and the Noble Laborer both, which meant I might already be guaranteed to fail.

Feeling introspective, I grabbed Sirlat's letter and retreated quietly to my chamber. For once, discussing a letter from Sirlat did not result in argument and condescension. Instead, I was left with questions, curiosity, and a desire to know more. I wanted to learn about the Noble Laborer and the natural state. I sat down upon my bed. I wanted to read Sirlat's letter.

For the first time in my life, I read what Sirlat had written me, from start to finish. She went to great lengths to insist that her beliefs were true and mine were false, arguing that because the state had chosen one faith, the Noble Laborer was likely to choose the other. I did not understand much of what she said—she twisted the facts in a way that made reality seem much more confusing than it was.

But to my surprise, Sirlat was neither angry, like Ansidrion, nor over-righteous, like Yhako. Instead, she was cordial, even loving. Why was she this way? We had never met, and she had scarcely heard a word from me. We were siblings, but only through blood, and not even our upbringings had been the same. Yet she called me her "dear brother, Federan," and remarked that she hoped to hear from me one day, although she would also be content in hearing of my success from others.

After I read the letter, I felt a bit of guilt that I had so thoroughly rejected Sirlat based entirely on what I had decided about her within my head. The true Sirlat was not the worst of both my brothers, as I had assumed, but instead a woman with such patience and grace that, despite my refusal to even acknowledge her, she continued to love me and write kind words to me. I still felt conviction that, despite her intelligence, Sirlat was wrong in her beliefs, but I finally, for the first time, had to recognize that she was a person. She had faults and strengths, but she also had emotions and values. I thought about Mother's final instruction, to honor and respect Sirlat.

I intended to undertake the challenge of the Noble Laborer, but Sirlat weighed far more heavily on my mind at that moment. Something I had taken as fact my entirely adolescence—Sirlat's smug obstinacy—had evaporated, yet although I felt guilty, I also felt at peace with the change.

It was a strangely temperate day; an oasis of spring warmth in the midst of a cold, snowy winter. I felt serene, and this feeling led me to believe that there might be a great change at work. I rested my head upon my pillow and closed my eyes, and the world fell silent. My mind was confused enough that I did not expect instant sleep, yet I felt peaceful enough that it came anyway.

I dreamt that Sirlat had returned home, and she scolded Yhako, Ansidrion, and me all for having quarreled in her absence. Yet I did not feel ashamed, but instead as though everything had been righted, and the four of us took a meal together. Then a comely, simple man with a smooth voice and sturdy accent appeared at our door, and Sirlat introduced him as the Noble Laborer, and we hailed him and treated him to a new shirt. I felt no urgency to ask him about universal truth, but instead I encouraged him to speak of his own life, and his words put me at ease. Yet, although he spoke in an open, frank manner, describing no detail that was not absolutely relevant, I found later that I could not recall for certain a single thing he had said.

The sleep was not heavy, and I frequently traveled in and out of consciousness. This transience lured me into believing that the dream was reality. Even after I fully awoke, and saw that what would have needed many hours did not even take one, I could not shake the lucidity of the experience. I continued to be haunted by the excitement of an upcoming arrival and the satisfaction of all of my curiosities, before the excitement shriveled, and I remembered that I expected something that might never happen. Why had I thought so much of Sirlat, anyway? She had never been an authority to me, never had any influence over me. I had only just read the whole of one of her letters for the first time in a decade! She should have been worthless to me, but I could not shake her gentle admonition: "You are a man now, Federan, and you must begin to undertake manly pursuits." Why did I put any value in this?

Determined that I should escape this false vision's grasp, I dressed myself in my coat and went outside for a walk. I marched toward Maidia Street, which was the primary host of calming walks for most Ilepyans. It was dusk now, and I wanted an hour or so to allow something else to run my mind. I tried to think about the distant holy city of Portavamqha and imagine what it must look like. I intended to make a pilgrimage there one day, and wanted to test the prophecy that anyone of true faith in the Order would already know the exact landscape and layout of the city. I had always wanted to carefully diagram a map to bring with me.

Yet, try as I might, I could not keep my focus. Sirlat persisted, refusing to leave my mind. On the street in one instant I thought I recognized the Noble Laborer from my dream, but then his face changed entirely, and he became a stuffy old man with a turned-up nose. I chose a verse from the Song of Galmosto and recited it in my head. Then I repeated it, this time in Portavan. But my mind continued to drift, and I found myself thinking about my brothers' rejection of the Lords' Occult to which the song belonged. I remembered how we had argued over it once, and how Sirlat might now disapprove. Her name kept rising in my mind. Maidia Street was full of people, come to celebrate this beautiful winter night, and yet I found that they could not distract me from my dream. Then I heard one of them say "Sirlat," and then another and another, until it was all I could hear. I had gone mad! I turned for home, knowing that Maidia Street was no place for a fool like me to wander. I despaired of ever setting my mind free again.

When I arrived at our home on Trafgha Street, total darkness had fallen but, as always, there was candlelight coming from within the home. Ansidrion would have gone to bed, and Yhako was certainly looking at his books and accounts, ensuring that all of the day's orders had been filled. But when I walked in the door, Sirlat's name still echoing through my ears, I found Yhako and Ansidrion both in the front parlor, and neither with work before him. Yhako looked despondent, perhaps with tears in his eyes. Just as I entered the house, Ansidrion had grabbed a vase and smashed it against the wall directly to my right. "How can he do such a thing? How will he not be punished for it?" But then he trained his eyes upon me. "And what have you to do with this?"

I frowned. "To do with what? I know nothing of what you speak." I looked to Yhako. "What has happened?"

Finally, a tear appeared beneath Yhako's eye and began down his face. "Word has come this night from Grontinion. Sirlat has died."

"Died?" Ansidrion shouted. "She has been killed at the hands of that criminal, that accursed man, Grontinion's Bishop Irat."

I could say nothing in response. I felt strange, empty, as though my body and soul were not in union. I heard the words, but I did not believe them. I sat down on the floor and said nothing for several minutes. I ceased to experience anything, and for a time I was as lifeless as a stone, having neither feeling nor thought.

I became animate again as I saw Ansidrion pound his fist upon a small table. He struck it with such force and soul that it splintered, and he growled in rage. Suddenly I realized that I did not feel great anger. I did not even feel sorrow, for although Sirlat and I had been given life by the same woman, I had never known her but through Yhako and Ansidrion's claims. She could have been dead my whole life, for she only existed through the legends recounted by those around me. No, I was not upset; I was mystified. I had only opened my heart to her that afternoon, to find that she had already left this world. Had the dream been a vision supplied by her? Had her spirit come to me, sensing that I was for the first time willing to receive it? I felt confused and tormented, and even guiltier at having never written her a letter. It was too late for me to do anything now.

"How can he think he will escape this?" Ansidrion demanded of Yhako. "Does he believe that the Order dictates that he slay the innocent?"

Yhako shook his head. He was quiet for a moment, and then said "it is about money." I looked up at him and Ansidrion fell silent. "Some men will stand for any manner of insult, but will not tolerate a threat to their coin. The bishops know that reform will take away their privileges, their ability to sell anything to poor believers in search of protection under the Order. Sirlat had spoken out against the corruption of the church. She decried the bishops who at every chance would gladly deprive a pound of gold from a beggar even if it only meant an ounce for themselves. The dishonorable Bishop Irat knew that, if Sirlat had her way, the false prophets would not maintain the great power through which they take great wealth. That bishop has made an example of Sirlat, that any man or woman who speaks out against the corruption of the church shall meet his or her end. Yet we know that to ignore it is to be complicit."

Ansidrion stood silent for a moment longer, fuming in anger. Then he turned back to me. "What think you of your holy Iqharepur now?" He seethed. "What will you say when he stands by the man who has had your sister murdered?"

I glared at him, stunned. This was not about me. It was not even about the Iqharepur. It was about the cruel, evil actions of one man, and no one else bore the responsibility. "The Iqharepur has done nothing wrong. He will not praise the crimes of this false man; do not seek to cast blame upon him."

"Is that so?" Ansidrion sneered. "Will the Iqharepur equivocate on a man whom his predecessor had appointed, and whose crime was to kill a woman who loathed the Iqharepur? And what will you say when days and weeks pass by and no condemnation comes?"

"I do not believe it shall be thus." I shrugged. Why did he attack me so? I did not defend Bishop Irat.

"How many innocent people must be killed by the Iqharepur's appointed before you will denounce him? Sirlat did nothing wrong, but was killed by power given from the Iqharepur! If the Iqharepur understands the Order best of all, then he would have known that Irat was capable of cruelty. Yet he appointed him anyway. Cursed be the name of the Iqharepur in this house! When must he finally have to take responsibility for his actions?"

"But Sirlat was not innocent," I replied. The argument slipped from my mouth before I had time to consider it. In fact, I knew Ansidrion was correct on some counts. The Iqharepur was hailed as an all knowing, unquestioned authority. Should he not ultimately bear responsibility for this? In any case, an accusation against the victim could not have been the best thing to offer at this time.

"Not innocent?" Ansidrion glared at me. "How 'not innocent?' What could Sirlat possibly have done to warrant murder?"

"I do not believe that Sirlat deserved what happened," I explained. "No one earns murder. But it is not as though the Bishop was not provoked. Sirlat harassed him at every turn; she spoke out against him and urged the people of Grontinion to resist him. Sirlat has made Grontinion unsafe for Bishop Irat with her threats. You all have boasted plenty of that."

"If Grontinion were not already unsafe for the wretched bishop, so now he has endangered himself," Yhako interjected. "For the people shall not now tolerate that criminal to live amongst them."

"And then, when he is murdered, who shall carry the blame?" Ansidrion asked. "It can only be the accursed Iqharepur, who through corruption has permitted all of this to happen."

I could not stomach any more of this. I did not support murder and I did not believe that what Bishop Irat did was right. But to treat Sirlat as some innocent martyr, and the Iqharepur as fully complicit, was outrageous. I refused to be present for it.

Having no other place to go, I fled to my bed, thoughts of the day's events thundering in my mind. I could make no sense of any of it; I needed to discuss it, but with someone who might be steadier, like Ma't. Now was not the time, of course—the old priest would surely be asleep at this hour—but I decided that the instant I saw a ray of light peer in through the window, I would rise and seek his wisdom.

To my surprise, I was able to scavenge a few bits of sleep from the night, but they cannot have been particularly restful. I dreamt of Sirlat and of Bishop Irat, of Yhako and Ansidrion, and I woke up several times with sweat escaping all parts of my body. I could not recall any of these dreams, only that they were haunted by the characters that had dominated my evening. Finally, when the sun began to rise some five hours before noon, I hastily dressed myself and stole out of the house. The night had provided no answers, no calm. My brain remained full of questions, and I knew that only Ma't could answer them.

The dark temple on Eparam Street was quiet, but there was a candle lit within, as the winter dawn did not provide sufficient light. I found Ma't in his chamber speaking quietly with another old man, but when he saw me, he shooed the man away. "Young Fe'n, be seated," he grunted, smiling as usual. "What brings you here unannounced?"

"I am sorry if I have come at an unexpected hour, Ma't," I began, my voice slow but firm. "But have you heard the word from Grontinion?"

Ma't frowned. "Grontinion? What filth comes from that loathsome place now?"

"I have received word that some of Bishop Irat's men have murdered my eldest sister, Sirlat." I attempted to remain constant and casual, in order to evoke neutrality from the priest.

But neutrality was not something Ma't ever valued. "So they have finally stopped the heretic, have they?" He grinned, as though it were natural and obvious to be cheerful about such an event.

I was not so convinced that my sister's death was cause for cheer, although I maintained the evenness in my tone. "But this is murder, is it not?"

"Yes, you could call it that, but certainly this murder is warranted for all that she has done."

"But is it not wrong?" I asked. "Has the Order not created all people? What the Order has created, nothing shall destroy."

"If it has happened, so the Order has willed it. The Order destroys evil things every minute, often through the agency of righteous men."

I sighed.

Suddenly, a terrible passion appeared in his eyes. "Think of this: Sirlat and the heretics seek to lead people away from the Order, into falsehood, do they not?"

I had to agree that they did, although more than ever, I had begun to believe that it was out of confusion, rather than evil design.

"And it is certain that Sirlat has helped lead dozens, perhaps hundreds of people astray from the Order. Do you believe this?"

"Yes, I suppose it is true."

"And think of how many more people Sirlat might have led from the Order if she had lived another ten or twenty years." Ma't's voice was tight and enthusiastic, and he rose to his feet. "Think of how many hundreds or thousands might have disrupted the Order if Sirlat were allowed to live! Bishop Irat has prevented it!" He leaned in, inches from my face. "In stopping one woman, he has saved a thousand! Indeed, the only reason I have not yet reported your brothers to the Bishop is because fighting against them has kept you resolute in our cause. Yet I can think of few deeds more honorable under the Order than to put a stop to such miseducation."

"But heretic though she was, Sirlat still had feelings. She was a human being, capable of pain and sorrow. How can it be right to put an end to her which the Order has not wrought directly?"

"Well then what would you suggest?" The old priest shrugged. His mouth opened into a smile, and his tongue peaked out from between the old, yellowed teeth.

"Can Bishop Irat not merely use his words? If his faith was superior—and I believe it was—could he not convince Sirlat through reason? For if Sirlat were capable of leading a thousand men into falsehood, could the Bishop not just as easily lead a thousand to truth?"

Ma't clapped his hands so abruptly, and with such force, that I jumped. "Fe'n, my boy! So young, so naïve! You have tried those same tactics with your brothers for years, and what has it yielded? Nothing yet, for they still actively preach heresy toward you. Think how much more difficult it would be with Sirlat, who hated her opponent and who was of much harder head than Yhako or Ansidrion?"

I sighed and my head fell. I did not want it to be true. But how could I argue? And then I remembered what Sirlat had written to me. The Noble Laborer! Would the world not be happier if we left it up to that peaceful being? Could we not put aside our acts of violence and hatred, leaving it to his unblemished discretion? After we found him we could live in unity, but until then, could we not be content in the knowledge that there was no certainty? Could there be peace if only everyone carried a small doubt?

Before I could voice this idea, Ma't began to speak again in that high, quick voice. "Come, Fe'n! I shall show you!" He made for the door, cane in hand.

"But Ma't." I tried to stop him. "What know you of the Miracle of the Noble Laborer?"

"There will be time for that later," he called, already nearly outside. "Come with me, boy!"

I did not want to follow him, but I was curious to see what he would do. I stood up and walked quickly after him. He was halfway down the street when I caught up, walking at such a fast pace despite his limp that remaining at his side left me short of breath. "Ma't, where do we go? Why do you walk so quickly?"

"I shall show you exactly where we mean to go!" He continued at his impossible pace, and I began to lag behind once again. He rounded a corner and I was nearly an entire minute late of him. And then I saw him speaking with a man of about Ansidrion's age, standing in the street. Before I had come within earshot of them, Ma't placed a few coins into the man's hand. "The rest are at my home," I heard the priest say. "Let us go now!" And then Ma't turned back down the way we came, passing me, as the man, and then I, followed. Our new companion wore a meek, plain smile upon a smooth complexion. His clothes were modest—he certainly was not a beggar, but I could see that the clothing had been worn for many days without having been washed. He walked calmly, and had the most upright posture I had ever seen. I wanted to ask Ma't what was happening, if he knew the man, but I found myself too curious to act. Nothing seemed like the right question to ask, and I knew that Ma't meant to teach me something, and so would not be presently forthcoming with details.

The two men said nothing to one another until Ma't stopped at the door to the temple. "The coin is inside," he explained, smiling. "Now as I said, this is all for a little wager I have with my friend." He pointed to me and nodded. The upright man looked my way and I forced a smile. "He believes that men of your generation are fools, but I know you to be wise, and therefore I shall give you a *bavdiyar* coin for every question you answer properly. Do you understand?"

"Yes, sir." The man nodded, his voice deep and frank.

"Very well, let us begin. Do you believe in and go in the path of the Order?"

The man shrugged. "Yes, naturally."

"Good, good." Ma't seemed to dance with excitement, but I could not figure out what was happening. "And how often do you attend instruction from a priest?"

"But at New Year, sir."

"It is fine, it is fine!" The old priest confirmed. "You seem to be the perfect candidate for this little bet. Tell me, boy: what know you of a Midnight Ritual?"

The man frowned, his thick eyebrows gathering to meet in the midst of his forehead. "I do not know, sir."

"That is no worry!" Ma't's eyes shone with excitement. "Let us on to the next one. Can you name the Seven Lords of the Occult?"

The upright man frowned again. "There is Galmosto, of course. And Ringellen is one, is he not? And..." he trailed off in attempted recollection. "That is all I know, sir."

"Two is not bad! And do you know any doctrine?"

"Doctrine?"

"Yes, religious documents. Letters written by bishops or the Iqharepur on important issues of the Order."

No, it could not be! I knew these questions. How did Ma't know them? Was this the Noble Laborer? Yes, it was the only explanation! Perhaps these questions were a well-known test, and Ma't had led me directly to the man. My heart began to flutter with joyful anticipation. I did not know what Ma't intended to do with the comely man with the smooth voice and sturdy accent, but I felt that something incredible, even miraculous, was about to happen.

"No bishop has ever written to me, if that is what you mean to ask!" The man laughed. "No, no doctrine, sir."

"That is good!" Ma't was still as excited as ever. "Come in and you will sign your name. Then the coin will be yours."

The man shrugged and smiled. He looked at me and I returned his glance, just as confused as he was. We walked into the temple together.

Ma't produced a small paper, and a straw and ink. The man managed a few letters. *Pelatt*, he wrote.

I said it aloud.

"That is my name, sir," he said. I smiled at him. I had to find a way to bring this man to Yhako.

Ma't retreated to the back of the room and then, true to his word, returned holding a few *bavdiyar* in his hand. "Put out your hand, boy," he commanded Pelatt. The man grinned and did what he was told, and the coins fell into his hand.

"I shall eat for a month with these!" Pelatt exclaimed, his eyes full of light. "This is marvelous. Oh, thank you sir!"

But before he had time even to look up at the priest in gratitude, Ma't's heavy cane came battering down upon Pelatt's wrist, and the coins flew everywhere. I leapt backward. Pelatt fell to the ground. But that did not stop Ma't, who raised the cane once again and drove the point of it into the poor man's right leg. Pelatt shouted in pain. I shut my eyes as tightly as I could and turned away. I heard the cane crash down again, and the man screamed. I opened my eyes and the whole room seemed to be coming down around me. I turned to Ma't, flinching all along, and saw him lift his cane up in the air once more. He was laughing with pleasure, his eyes crazed and full of satisfaction. This was the most dreadful thing I had ever experienced. I had to do something to make it stop. I grabbed the old man's right arm and held it with all my might. "No, Ma't!" I cried. "No more!"

Ma't turned to me, still holding the cane with that wild look upon his face. I wrested the cane from his hand and threw it to the ground. His eyes gradually receded to their normal size, but the crooked old smile remained. Pelatt was still on the ground, one arm upon his head, the other clutching his leg. He was moving, groaning, and blood began to seep through the right leg of his trousers. "He is a heretic," Ma't explained, his words seemingly distant from one another; isolated by quick, shallow breaths of excitement. "It is as I have told you; we must protect the poor, innocent people from him."

But I could not shake the feeling that Ma't had just attacked the Noble Laborer. "What says to you he is a heretic? He is merely an uneducated man, but everything about him has suggested that his soul and heart are pure. We had only to instruct him properly."

"He stood in front of a suspected *deshilva* school, a heretic school. He knew nothing of the true doctrine. It is too late to educate him, for his mind has already been poisoned by the traitors. Now stand aside, that I may finish the task." He pulled free from my hand, but I grabbed him again before he could recover the cane. I held his feeble wrists together in my hand behind his back, and wrapped my left arm around his chest. His heart was beating furiously, and I could feel his lungs rapidly expand and contract.

"I shall not!" I insisted. "Pelatt, you must leave this place. I know you are badly injured, but you must get yourself home before worse befalls you. Seek comfort and care in the home of a friend if you must, as long as it is far from here!" I watched the man as he struggled to find his way to his feet. He stood upon his right leg, but it gave out, and he collapsed to the floor once again. "Take the cane," I instructed him, holding tight against Ma't's resistance. The old priest might have summoned all of his strength in his zeal to carry out this crime, but in the fight for what was right, I managed to be stronger. I knew that I could and would restrain Ma't for as long as was necessary to save this man.

Slowly, Pelatt managed to stand up once again, grasping the blooded point atop the wooden cane. It was a bit too short for him, and his once-perfect posture had now been replaced with a harsh slouch and a slow, pained gait. He groaned in agony each time he set his weight upon his right leg, but I knew he bore the injury with all of the strength and dignity he had. He looked back at me as he neared the door. "I am sorry," I told him, sighing. He cringed and hobbled from the building.

I knew it would take poor Pelatt some time before he managed to get to safety, so I continued to restrain Ma't, although he had stopped resisting. "You are allowing a heretic to go free, boy," he began to taunt me. "You are obstructing the path of the Order."

"Ma't, I have trusted you with the world, exactly as Mother instructed. But this day, you have not done the work of the Order."

We remained there for several minutes more, as Ma't attempted to shame me into releasing him. But I remained steadfast, holding him firm for what seemed an eternity. Then, abruptly, I let him loose and he stumbled to the ground. Without his cane, walking would be difficult, and I had no idea when another friend or pupil might come to him to aid his stroll, but I did not care. I left as soon as I let him loose, although he continued to shout at me. "You will return unto me! You will see the error in this!"

I walked the streets for an hour, searching for signs of noble Pelatt. There were a few spots of ruddy dirt that led west toward Turka Street, and then a few more that pointed north. But then they disappeared, and I had no clue as to where he might have gone. I returned to the *deshilva* school where Ma't had first located him, but the men within knew no one by his name, and he was not amongst the wards that slept there.

I knew that Pelatt was gone, and that my one opportunity with the Noble Laborer had been lost. But I did not want to go home. I felt as though so much had changed since I had last seen Yhako and Ansidrion, since I had defended the Iqharepur against their insults. Would I defend him now? Everything seemed to have shed its old value in a day, although I had yet to discover its new meaning.

I had no other choice, however. Unlike my escape from the *deshilva* school, Ma't and the church offered me no respite. No, there was no place I might go except for my own home. Having felt so traumatized by the day's events, however, I vowed not to speak to my brothers at all, but rather to retreat from them as quickly as I could. The two men were sitting in the parlor when I returned, shouting and ranting as they had the day before. Ansidrion called to me when I entered, perhaps preparing to curse the Iqharepur once over, but I ignored him and made for my bed.

There was little I wanted more than sleep at that moment, but it eluded me. I should have been exhausted after the morning I had had, and the night before it, but there was no escaping my thoughts. I at once felt that I loathed everyone: Sirlat, the bishop who had her killed, Yhako and Ansidrion, and Ma't. They had all shattered my peace, forcing me to come to terms with a new and unwelcome realm, in which nothing was as I had planned it.

But more than any of them, I thought of Pelatt. Sirlat's murder had set into motion events that led to such a brutal attack on this innocent, unrelated man. How could faiths, which should serve only to give truth and succor, harm so many? I knew that something was wrong with this. I knew that, unwelcome as it was, this challenge to my beliefs was necessary.

And then, suddenly, I realized that I would have to speak with Yhako. I could remain in my bed, hoping for these great changes to undo themselves, but at heart I knew that they never could. I realized that I faced two possibilities: either the peace among brothers and sisters that Sirlat had offered in my dream, or the violence and destruction that the Priest and Bishop had offered in reality. The dream appealed to me, of course, and in spite of all that had happened, it seemed more in reach than before. But it was something I would have to work toward, or the violent destruction would continue.

I remained in my room until night had fallen, so as to avoid Ansidrion. He was sure to meet me with passion, and I was not prepared for it. So, once he had gone to bed, I went to the office, where Yhako spent most of his nights. However, news of Sirlat's death had so consumed him that the business interested him very little, and instead I found him in the study. "Yhako," I said softly as I stood at the doorway.

"Federan? I do not expect to see you at this hour. What is it?"

I entered the study, but maintained my distance. "I have met the Noble Laborer." I stopped, waiting for a reaction. Yhako merely raised his eyebrows, to signal for me to continue. Accepting this, I recounted to him the events of the previous day, explaining my firm belief that the man I met was the man from the miracle I had heard less than two days before. "He was an innocent man—a good man, and Ma't intended to kill him." My eyes became wide and my breath heavy as I finished telling of the events that still tortured me. Even so, Yhako was silent, his face betraying nothing. So I admitted what I had to. "I do not trust Ma't. I do not intend to see him again."

Finally, Yhako spoke. "I am sorry for what has befallen your friend. But I am glad that it has caused you to see the truth."

"I cannot say that I am prepared to believe as you and Ansidrion do, only that I can no longer follow a belief that permits violence and unkind acts against anyone."

"That is sufficient, Federan. You may believe whatever you wish."

"Very well. Then where would you advise I begin? Now that my mind is open anew, I would like to study with you, to see if it has value to me."

Yhako thought for a moment. I expected to take my seat there next to him and begin reading over a thesis or book from our library, as he did. But, to my surprise, this is not what he suggested. "Go and find Sirlat's letters. Let you read them, and let you reflect and decide what you believe."

So, without a response, I returned to my chamber and gathered up a few of the letters my sister had written to me. I did not have them all—I had thrown many of them out, usually to show my brothers that they had no sway over me. But I had kept a dozen of them, and decided now to read them in the order that they had been written.

The first was from some five or six years ago, and Sirlat had included a few kind words for my thirteenth birthday, and condolences over Mother's death. Then she moved on to more substantive topics, but she did not speak directly of religion, as I had expected. Instead this letter—like most of the others, I was to learn—was political and philosophical in its content. I moved on to the next, and then read through most of the older ones. Slowly, I assembled the pieces of ideas from the many notes. In one, she had said:

> *Federan, I have no wish to compel you to my*
> *faith. Indeed, I am wary of anyone who would*
> *convince another of her religion by manner of*
> *force. I merely want you to understand how the*
> *political structure of your religion enables the*
> *oppression of many millions of people.*

And yet, in the missive previous to this, she had noted in passing that:

> *Times have never been better in Grontinion than*
> *they are today. We have succeeded in our*
> *revolution, and the people have won their freedom*
> *from tyrannical government. There remain a*
> *number of matters that we must sort out, but*
> *considering how far we have come, I am content.*

These statements did not seem to match, especially considering that Sirlat's assassination had been due to the politics of religion. How could she be content if she was wary of religious pressure in her own city—the very religious pressure that would soon cause her end? Perhaps faith did not matter as much to Sirlat as I thought it had. Perhaps her fight against Bishop Irat had not been an attempt to change the Bishop's religion, but instead to cause the Bishop to cease harming those who had already changed theirs. Sirlat had not fought under the flag of religious reform, but rather religious liberty.

I read the penultimate note—that which had described the death of the previous Iqharepur and the appointment of the next. But these were but minor details; Sirlat was much more concerned with the governing precedent that they set:

> *A person should be chosen to lead a people*
> *because she or he shows the greatest talent at it,*

and vision for it. Perhaps this young boy can become a great leader, but there is no reason to expect as much. Hereditary government, governance for life—it is all false and dangerous, and I fear for the people of Portavamqha who must live under it.

She was not the woman I had always assumed she was. I felt ashamed. I had spent years rejecting her, denouncing her, only based on a false idea of her life's work. Now I saw the brilliant woman Yhako and Ansidrion had always praised, and I felt sorrow that I had only realized it once it was too late to build a relationship with her.

There was only one more letter. It was the posthumous piece which I had read but two days before. But now I had a new perspective, and I wanted to read the entire tale in sequence. So I found Sirlat's recounting of the Noble Laborer and read it once more.

To my surprise, the letter seemed to be entirely different than I remembered it. It was as though the words had changed since I last laid eyes upon them, and although the major points were the same as before, they seemed to carry new, different meaning. It was not a question of faith at all. It closed by saying:

Think, if there is anyone capable of fairly arbitrating between the many religions, would she do so in your society? Would the Noble Laborer feel free in Ilepya or anywhere in Hihaythea to declare in favor of the faith the State opposed? There, then, you see the problem, for when the State chooses an ideology, no one is at liberty to find differently.

GUILTY NAMES

She made no argument in favor of her religion.
Rather, she merely wanted the same liberty for her to
pursue hers as I had to pursue mine. And given her
case—and what I had witnessed that day—I had no
means to dispute it. Had Ma't not acted as the very
manifestation of the State, influencing and silencing Pelatt
before he had a chance to respond?

I could not tolerate the idea of facing my brothers
knowing I had misjudged Sirlat. I wanted to remain in my
chamber for eternity, as losing my life for lack of
nourishment appealed more to me than admitting I had so
gravely erred.

But then I remembered what Sirlat had said in
one of the letters: "You are a man now, Federan, and you
must begin to undertake manly pursuits." I had no choice
but to go. At this hour Ansidrion would be awake as well,
perhaps breaking his fast. I wanted to confront my
brothers together, to avoid having to do the deed twice.
So I found Ansidrion—in the kitchen, as I had
expected—and I sat as he prepared some bread and
cheese. I chuckled silently at the poignancy of the
moment; I had undergone a major philosophical
transformation, but Ansidrion had no idea of it. Yhako at
least knew that some change was occurring within me,
although he had yet to know the result. The two of them
had greater things on their mind that morning, but I was
sure to claim my bit of attention.

Ansidrion and I said nothing to one another in
the kitchen. Then, realizing I owed him a few words, I
said "I am sorry for what has happened to Sirlat. It is a
cruel thing that has befallen her, and I condemn everyone
who is responsible for it."

But Ansidrion merely glanced up at me, shook his
head, and sneered. Then, he stared back down at his food
and continued eating in silence. He would be much harder
to win over than Yhako, but I suppose he deserved my

sympathy and patience at this hour for the death of his beloved sister.

I remained in the kitchen with Ansidrion as he finished eating in silence, and then I followed him to the study. He took his seat beside Yhako, who looked up at me with wide-eyed anticipation. "Have you read the letters? Have you spoken with Ansidrion on it?"

"Spoken with me on what, Federan?" Ansidrion snapped. "What letters?"

I took a deep breath. "My mind has been opened. I have read all of Sirlat's letters." I closed my eyes and breathed deep anew. "I have seen the wisdom, the truth to them. Having read her words—including those on the Noble Laborer—I see now how I have followed a system that has led to repression, and I renounce it now. I no longer follow the Iqharepur."

This last sentence I had not expected to utter. Indeed, even as recently as I sat in the kitchen beside Ansidrion, I had never even considered rejecting the Iqharepur. But having said everything I said before it, this seemed to be the only option. If this system had oppressed others, if it had caused Pelatt's assault and Sirlat's murder, then it was only right that the leader of the system be held accountable. I could not believe in the authority of the Iqharepur if I did not believe in the acts of his surrogates.

Ansidrion's mouth had fallen agape, and he was, for once, speechless. Yhako smiled. "That is good, Federan. If there is any way in which Sirlat's death might have wrought something positive, it is this."

I grinned, relieved. I felt, for the first time since those days in Maidia Square, at ease in the presence of my brothers. It was strange, new, and terrifying. But it also seemed right.

"So it has come from Sirlat's murder, then?" Ansidrion asked.

"Yes," I said. "At least, that has been a vital part of it." So I explained to him, as I had to Yhako, all that I had experienced over the last two days.

But to my surprise, Ansidrion was not immediately concerned with the outcome. As soon as he had his chance, he interjected on a nuance I had not expected. "Why do you say you have met the Noble Laborer when you have not?"

I was stunned. "I believe I have, Ansidrion. How can you say I have not when you do not know?"

"It is impossible for you to have met him," he countered. "Sirlat herself said that the Noble Laborer likely cannot even exist! You have just met a man on the street and claimed that he is someone, ascribed him an identity, without any evidence."

I looked to Yhako and shrugged. Yhako took up my cause. "If he says he has met the Noble Laborer, we shall trust him. Besides, this is not the most important detail, Ansidrion. Masbat has attacked that poor man. It has allowed Federan to see the truth."

Ansidrion sighed. "Very well, if it has a good outcome, I shall let it pass. I am glad you have joined us, Federan. You have much to learn."

I had not expected such a rebuke from my brother at this hour, but we had many years of mutual hostility behind us. It was not so easy to erase all of it. He was grieving, besides, and given time, he would surely open to my overtures.

Yhako, likely sensing that I had fallen slightly disheartened, invited me to sit at his desk with him. "I am very proud of you, Federan. You have done well, and I predict that we have many bright days before us."

"Thank you, Yhako. I would like to believe so as well. But I suppose the time has come for me to begin. Shall I study with you this morning?"

"Perhaps it is best if you begin learning different languages, so that you are able to understand the many foreign papers we study. You can read in Galmostan, of course, but what other tongues do you know?"

"I have taught myself Portavan during my days with Ma't, but I have not been able to learn anything else."

"Very well, I can show you Gringellic, the language of the University of Grontinion. It is similar to Galmostan, so it should not be too difficult.

"A bright young man like Federan can pick it up with ease," Ansidrion chimed in.

"Gringellic it will be," Yhako agreed. He began at once to teach me the letters and tell me the sounds, and explain how words were constructed. The language was complex, but once I understood its patterns, after several hours, I made progress at it. "You have a talent for languages," Yhako told me. "If we spend this much time at it each day, I believe you will be fluent within a short time."

"I hope so, for I am sure there are many important texts that I might only read in this language."

"Indeed there are. But now we have come to the end for this day."

"During these short winter days, Federan, when the sunlight is so hard to come by, we only study during the midday hours," Ansidrion explained. "The eyestrain garnered from studying by candlelight might tempt you now, but we shall regret it in later years. There will be plenty of time to study tomorrow and in the days ahead; for now, let us take a meal together."

I followed my brothers to the kitchen, where I placed the dishes on the table as they prepared the food. "Salted meat today, at last!" Ansidrion grinned. In winter, game was scarce enough that we could only eat it one meal a week, and Ansidrion relished these days more than any others.

"I await late spring, when we might have meat again every day," I said, smiling.

Ansidrion took his seat. "I wish the time would come sooner than that." Abruptly, his face and tone became serious. "It has not always been this way. It will not always be this way."

"If we are truthful, abstaining from meat a few days out of the week is not such a tragedy," I said.

"No, you are right about that. But there are many households in Ilepya that cannot eat well, even in the spring and at harvest time. Most homes have empty cupboards and bare tables from winter's end to its start again."

"Ilepya is in crisis now," Yhako explained. "There are fewer goods flowing into and out of the city than ever before, and although we might not feel it because the *as'shelik* business carries on, most people here are suffering more than they have, and more than others do in other places."

"And why is that?" I asked. "What has caused this city to founder?"

"There are many causes, as always," Yhako continued. "But I believe that it has largely come as a result of our poor governance, of those in power taking more from those in need than ever they have."

"You have said that the government chooses our beliefs for us, by giving the religious hierarchy and its police authority and allowing them to stifle opposing ideas. But how else are we misruled?" I asked.

"If you will, Federan, think of the Apgha, that great palace on Maidia Street," Yhako instructed. "Please recite to us the ways in which the deputies of the Bishop who resides there are present in daily life here in Ilepya."

"There is the police force, the *asdesaj*, of course," I began.

"And tell me, what you have seen them do?"

"They have shut down the school on Kalal Street. That is what I remember them most for. And on occasion they apprehend a criminal. And they have appeared at our door to collect taxes."

"Always with clubs in their hands," Ansidrion added.

"Yes, that has been the case," I agreed.

"When else?" Yhako pressed.

I thought for a moment. "That is the whole, as far as I can recall. I do not see the *asdesaj* at any other time."

"But think beyond the *asdesaj*. When have you seen any other manifestation of the government?"

I frowned. Government beyond the *asdesaj*? Perhaps he meant the religious structure. "I suppose their orders have come from the Bishop, and they have endorsed the priests, so therefore Ma't's actions have been an extension of the Apgha."

"Yes, that is true, although it is not what I suggest."

"Well then what do do you wish to hear? I have listed every action I have seen by the *asdesaj*."

"He cannot see any government beyond its hired force," Ansidrion said to Yhako.

"Yes, and that is exactly the issue," Yhako agreed. "Federan, the *asdesaj* is not the government. They are merely a force in the government's employ. And the government is able to pay the *asdesaj* through the imposts they collect on our business, meaning that both the government and the *asdesaj* rely on us for survival. They are paid indirectly by us."

"Wait, Yhako, you move too quickly. If the *asdesaj* is not the government, then what is?"

Yhako sighed. "It should not be this way. Our government seems only to be the Bishop and his will as it is imposed through force. But in other nations, such as Yafia and Colof, the laws are codified and cannot be violated or easily changed by those in power. Cities and countries are governed by mayors and representatives who are chosen by the people. The laws and taxes are regular and predictable and work toward the common good, rather than as subject to the arbitrary will of an autocrat for his own benefit."

I frowned. At this date, having never lived under anything other than a heavy-handed but disorganized theocratic dictatorship, I could not easily comprehend anything else.

Ansidrion took up the challenge once again. "Imagine if the current bishop were to die this night, and that tomorrow his successor ruled that the school on Kalal Street should open."

"That would be most welcome!" I responded. "And he might free the lecturers who were captured from there!"

"Yes, but then what if he were to die the next day, and were replaced again by a bishop who wanted the school closed anew, and all of its lecturers killed?"

"That would not be welcome, obviously. What do you mean by it?"

"That this arbitrariness, this lack of constancy, is what prevents the city from thriving. There are no laws here—merely the whims of the mighty Bishop and his armed henchmen. In these conditions there can be no trade, no business, no prosperity, no happiness. Every citizen must go in constant fear that the Bishop's will might abruptly turn against him."

"We need a law, Federan," Yhako interjected. "We need rules of the government, guarantees to the people as to how they will be treated. Today, no one can cross or question the Bishop, for he merely commands you that his will is that of the Order, and that to defy him is to defy the Order. So, by building such divine authority into the public structure, the people are made to believe that their oppression and suffering is an inevitable part of the Order."

I thought about Ma't's insistence that I not question the Bishop's intent to close the Kalal school. If the capture and punishment of so many people was determined by the indomitable Order, of course there was no fighting against it. But now I acknowledged that the awful events of that day, several years before, were wrong. The Bishop and my priest had been wrong, which our system could not account for. "It seems like a great change from what we have now."

"Yes," Ansidrion continued, "but it is not too much change at all. The money, the labor, and the confidence of the people are what sustain the Bishop. We must withdraw these from him, and cause him to fall, so that we can create the government we need."

"But the people in this city still provide these things to him. How do we convince them? How do we awaken them, as you both have said, to this oppression that they have never noticed?"

No one said anything for a moment. Then Yhako answered. "I suppose they must be stirred by some bold action, although I do not yet know what that is."

Suddenly, I remembered what Ma't had said about going after Yhako and Ansidrion. "What is to stop my old priest from telling our names to the Bishop, and sending the *asdesaj* unto us?"

"That priest has no power over us," Ansidrion scoffed. "We have always been safe from him."

"But the Kalal school...." No, I still could not tell them about my connection to that terrible crime. "We are heretics, traitors to the government. Who is to say they will not come after us with all of their might?"

Yhako shrugged. "There is nothing to stop them. This is a constant risk. Our lives are a challenge to those in power. But we must not choose to be ignorant, and to neglect a noble cause, merely out of caution."

I frowned. "Why have they not attacked us already? Our sister was known for her actions in Grontinion. Our parents were the sort of intellectuals who seemed to be created merely to question the government. We should have long ago been eradicated if the state is nearly as oppressive as you claim."

"They are oppressive, Federan. But they are not organized enough. There are dozens, perhaps hundreds of others like us in this city. The bishop cannot shut all of us down at once—it would be costly, unseemly, and would stifle their tax revenues. Instead, they attack one of us at a time, as they did to my friend the other day. The *asdesaj* could arrive at any moment, but they might never come."

"If only there were something to draw these hundreds of rebels together, in united action against the government," I said. "For united, the people are surely stronger than the Bishop and his small police force."

"They certainly are," Yhako agreed. "Yet again, we find ourselves asking how the people can be awakened, be brought together, to act as one body against their oppressors. But how would you?"

We were silent. I did not know. At the time, none of us did, although we each would soon attempt to bring the people together in our own way.

II

"We have lost a sibling, friend, and scholar, but her death has enabled us to make a great friend and scholar of our remaining sibling," Ansidrion told me one evening.

Without words to meet this surprising warmth, I could only offer an embarassed smile in response. I had continued to study religious and philosophical essays during the day, enjoying rousing political discussions with my brothers. Until that compliment from Ansidrion, statements about Sirlat had come in sorrow. "I wish our eldest sister could see how much you have grown, Federan," Yhako had said. But the mere mention of her name would cause both his and Ansidrion's eyes to well with pain and tears.

"On days such as this...." I began, but halted, knowing that I could say nothing to relieve their mourning. Hearing and thinking about Sirlat made me regret how much time I had wasted rejecting my brothers, for now that I enjoyed it, I could not imagine life without their friendship.

With this awakening, I rapidly began to adopt belief in real political reform. I thought about the tyranny and oppression in Ilepya and understood that we would have to establish a written law for those in power to follow. But Sirlat's murder did not only evoke a change in me. We received news several months later that Bishop Irat, himself, had been assassinated.

"Who has killed him?" I asked Ansidrion, who had read the news to us from a letter.

"A great movement of people came together in Grontinion and chased him out. He fled to Rakka, but the people there did not want him, either, and a mob of revolutionaries put him to an end. It is wondrous news!"

"But it is wrong, is it not?" I asked.

Ansidrion glared at me. "Wrong? Is it evil to remove a man who has done so many terrible things? He used his power to harm and kill the people. With his death the people of Grontinion and Rakka will be free."

I knew that I had had this conversation many times before, with Ansidrion and with Ma't. I had never convinced anyone from the argument, so I felt there was no use in rebuttal, but still I made my position known: "That may be true, but I do not believe his murder was proper."

Yhako intervened before we could descend into an unresolvable argument. "But Federan, you cannot doubt that good has come from his removal. The disestablishment of the state religion is the natural and necessary progression of the revolution, by which the people are afforded more and more personal freedoms. Can you imagine a victorious revolution here, in Ilepya, in which our bishop maintains his absolute power? It is incompatible."

"I suppose I should be joyful for the loosening of the grip that the church had on the people of Grontinion," I conceded. "Indeed, I am happy even as I am offended. So I suppose I should seek to bask in the joy, rather than wallow in the offense."

"Yes, and perhaps even better than the Bishop's stinking corpse is this," Ansidrion proclaimed, reading from the letter of one of Sirlat's old colleagues. "'The newly republican governments of Yafia and Colof have pledged and will commence to implore the Dictator and magistrates of Hihaythea to adopt a constitution and grant the people more rights.'"

"But they will never!" I interjected.

"'And if they do not, the governments of Yafia and Colof shall encourage the Hihaythean people directly.'"

"What does that mean?" I asked.

"It is a wonderful threat if ever I have heard one," Ansidrion said.

"Our Dictator is isolated now," Yhako explained. "Colof and especially Yafia were our closest allies. Yet now we can expect them to subvert our government."

"But *how*?" I demanded. "This wonderful threat sounds entirely empty to me."

"Perhaps it is," Yhako conceded. "I cannot imagine a military invasion. But I do not know what else might accomplish anything."

But our neighboring nations must have settled on something. Within a few months, we began to see growing evidence of dissent. Ansidrion found an anti-government pamphlet on the streets one afternoon. Yhako brought word that one of his friends had met with a trio of Yiffen agents who were living in Ilepya. Then we heard that several people had been arrested and accused of throwing rocks at the Apgha Palace at night. Finally, there was a *tarbhasht*, or labor strike by the port workers. It was quickly broken up and brutally put down, but it was clear to us that the people of Ilepya were slowly stirring from their apathy. It was possible, if one listened carefully enough, to hear people on the streets whispering about the need for our Bishop to be dealt with as the Yiffens had with Irat.

None of these actions managed to bring about any change in government. "In a repressive system like ours, any of it is bound to lead to imprisonment or death," Yhako said ominously.

"But all movements must start somewhere," I responded.

But for the Ponyhubiresh brothers, things remained the same. There was no battle against the Bishop and the *asdesaj* in the streets, and even if there had been, we were scholars, not warriors. We had no business attempting to overthrow a government. We cheered the others, of course, and Yhako and Ansidrion gladly circulated the pamphlets to everyone they trusted, but we took no means to escalate the action.

Events might have continued along on this path, with us allowing this small chatter to blossom into a movement around us, had Yhako not brought home news one day that irrevocably changed it all. He had no idea. None of us could have. When he announced that one of his old friends had started a cabal of revolutionaries called the Ilepyan Brotherhood, he told of it innocently enough. "I plan to offer them a modest financial backing, a gesture to show our support for revolution. Perhaps fifty *bavdiyar* a month, do you think? Nothing large enough to be traced back to us."

"Make it fifty five," Ansidrion instructed.

"Why not sixty?" I asked. "Our household has accumulated a substantial amount of wealth, and the three of us have very little use for it. Let it go to a cause such as this."

So we settled the matter without debate, and then, as I was feeling slightly ill of the stomach, I excused myself and retired to bed early. When I awoke the following morning, my condition improved, I went to the study to join my brothers as I always did. To my surprise, neither of them was present. I searched their bedchambers but they were not therewithin either, so I assumed they had left on some errand and would return shortly. I thought very little of it, and found a bite of bread and sat down at my desk.

About an hour later, Yhako entered the home alone. "You are here, brother." I smiled at him. "But now what have you done with Ansidrion?"

"That man," he said, shaking his head. I could not say if he was upset, although I sensed conflict in his voice and countenance. "That man shall go his own way."

"Which way is this? Where is he?"

"I have taken him to see an old acquaintance, Edoro Beinsar, the cobbler. He is at Beinsar's house at present, deciding what to do with the rest of his life."

"Do not tell me Ansidrion has chosen to forsake us for shoes!" I still could not read Yhako's emotions, so I attempted to keep the tone light.

"He has decided to join the Ilepyan Brotherhood. Or, perhaps he has decided not to. Who is to say? But the idea so enchanted him that he could speak of nothing more than it last night, and refused even to sleep, pestering me as I took up the *as'shelik* books. He so wore me down that I had no choice but to agree to take him to see Beinsar this morning to discuss membership in the group."

"Oh, that is quite a surprise," I admitted. "Of course he is strongly interested in revolutionary activity. And that he has made the decision and then immediately acted upon it does not shock me, either. He has not a moment's patience in him, and as soon as he sets his mind to something, he cannot be led astray. But to join the Brotherhood?"

Yhako shrugged.

"Yes, of course he wants change," I continued. "We all want change. But participating in a revolutionary organization is uncharted territory for any of us. It frightens me, Yhako. Does it not frighten you?"

"Between you and me, and I suppose between him and me as well, I hope he decides against it. He is far too lacking in caution to be putting his life at risk so."

"I agree. When placed in a dangerous situation, he is too likely to press forward. Besides, not only does it bring great risks upon him, it also endangers our family. If he were to be caught, what is to prevent those in power from coming after either of us?"

Of course, there was no putting Ansidrion off, and I knew it. When he returned home that afternoon, Yhako and I were sitting in the study, having pretended to labor all day. I thought of nothing but Ansidrion and the great risk he was taking. I knew Yhako well enough to know that he could not study in this state either, and I hoped that he had spent the day thinking on how to trick Ansidrion out of joining the Brotherhood. That was our only hope. Ansidrion could not be dissuaded directly, but Yhako, in all of his wisdom, might be able to fool him away.

So I waited in expectation, hoping that every word in the conversation to come was part of a great game Yhako had planned. "And what will you have decided?" He began casually.

"The Brotherhood meets one night each week. I shall attend my first meeting two nights hence." Ansidrion smiled, appearing very pleased with himself.

"Then you will join them?"

"It is so. The Brotherhood will be the only way anything is accomplished in this city. With my membership and your financial support, we might actually manage a revolution." Then he looked at me. "You might consider accompanying me, Federan."

"Me? I remain new to this movement, far too innocent of it all to be taking such action," I sputtered. "I have studying to do, knowledge to acquire before becoming so involved." The idea seemed abrupt, and it terrified me.

Ansidrion likely was not convinced, but Yhako steered the conversation away from the topic. "And your

GUILTY NAMES

sleep?" He asked. "How will you rest on those nights if you are to attend meetings?"

"These are exciting times, Yhako! A man does not need sleep; fighting for revolution is invigorating enough!"

Yhako frowned for a moment, and then merely shrugged. "I suppose it is so."

Ansidrion glanced at both of us, but I avoided his gaze, wary that he might suggest my membership again. Then he left the room, allowing me a chance to interrogate Yhako.

"Will you do nothing about this? He puts himself, he puts us in danger, and his sleep is all you caution?"

"Of course there is danger, Federan. But he will not be put off. You cannot understand how deeply he is drawn to this."

I heard a bit of desperate exhaustion in Yhako's voice, but I would not give in so easily. "And what if he convinces me to attend meetings with him? Would you simply allow me to join the Ilepyan Brotherhood as well?"

"No, Federan. It is not for you, and you know it. There will be no need in convincing you not to join, because you will have already convinced yourself."

"But for Ansidrion?"

"Ansidrion throws himself down a path, hastening toward an end. Once he has an outcome in mind, one can only delay him, but there is no dissuasion."

"Then delay him! Give him obstacles, prevent him from attending even if but for a week or two. Perhaps it will give him enough time between now and then to change his mind."

"No, he wants this more than anything else. I saw it in his eyes last night, this morning, and this afternoon now. He is already envisioning himself in the Ilepyan Brotherhood, taking radical action. There is no purpose in delaying it."

I wanted to argue more, but I sensed in Yhako what he saw in Ansidrion. He was an immovable force, unwilling to alter events from the motion into which they had now been set.

I remained in a state of constant tension the next two days. I could do nothing without thinking of the Ilepyan Brotherhood and the sort of danger it posed, but I also refused to mention it in conversation, hoping that if it were not spoken, it would disappear. So I sat in front of books and documents, reading sentences and then forgetting what they had said, my mind deeply distracted.

For their part, Yhako and Ansidrion pretended to interact normally, although both of them were clearly affected by the situation as well. Ansidrion was full of excitement, of course, constantly smiling and speaking much more quickly than usual. He was loud, restless, energetic. Perhaps if I had had more grace, I might have been happy for him and all of his boundless excitement.

Yhako, however, seemed to be experiencing the opposite. He was tired, and his words were quiet and slow. He spoke very little and seemed as distracted as I was. When I asked him about it, he dismissed my concerns. "There are troubles with the *shelik* business," he claimed. "It will clear up shortly, and nothing will then bother us."

When the time came for Ansidrion to attend the first meeting, I retreated to my bed early. I was fearful that he might again suggest that I come along, so I avoided him altogether. I had trouble sleeping, naturally, but with the aid of the sweet root tea that my brothers drank, I managed to doze a bit. I tossed and turned the night through, and when I did sleep, my mind was haunted by dreams of the police, the *asdesaj*, appearing at our door and searching through our belongings.

The next morning, I was relieved to find both of my brothers in the study. Yhako seemed even more exhausted than he had been the night before, while Ansidrion appeared fresh and youthful. "Good morning, *dofit!*" He called to me. "How have you slept?"

"Imperfectly," I replied, and took my seat. I was upset with Ansidrion, but I also felt some relief that he had defied my expectations and survived the first meeting.

"I am sorry for that, although between the three of us, you still caught the most rest this night!"

I ignored this, and instead turned the conversation to the obvious. "And your night? I suppose there must be something to say in its regard?"

"Federan, I enjoyed it. I believe in it. I shall attend every meeting hence." He was beaming, obviously imagining himself at upcoming gatherings. "I know that it is these men, these revolutionaries, who will bring about the great change we need, and I am pleased to now be among them."

This was not what I had wanted to hear at all. "How? What will they do?"

"They have posed some ideas, but nothing is planned for certain yet. It is too soon to worry you with what we might do, but the Brotherhood has a clear vision for Ilepya, and will not be put off from achieving it."

"Then it sounds as though you belong, for I see the same in you. But I worry that the *asdesaj* will likewise not be put off from stopping you."

"Oh come, *dofit*. There is no harm in meeting and discussing solutions to the problems of the world. I believe it is the least we can do at this date."

"I see plenty of harm. You could be caught and killed by those who wish for nothing more than to stifle all dissent."

"You are correct. I could be killed. But this small risk to my safety is a sacrifice worth the reward it could bring to all people. It is exactly the sort of bold action through which a revolution might be brought about."

I scoffed. "I never expected that you might hazard your safety so!"

"No, let the hard work come from others," he mocked me. "If we are to expect that others sacrifice for our good, then we should be willing to sacrifice for others as well."

I had no response. I did not feel that his words were correct, yet I could not find where he had erred. Was it really right that a good man such as Ansidrion risk his life for this cause? I wanted it to be wrong, but that did not make it so.

The following week, however, I felt less consternation as Ansidrion prepared to leave. "I suppose if you have survived one meeting, perhaps it is not a curse upon you and our family," I told him. "May you have a safe and productive evening."

"From you, Federan, I might expect no better wishes. My evening will be far more productive with the Brotherhood than any night spent idly in the house."

I waved him off and went to join Yhako for a cup of tea. Yhako was in the study, poring over religious and political theses. "Is it not time yet to take up the *as'shelik* books?" I asked.

"There is still an hour or so before I must move on to that task. Business has been slow lately, besides." A great yawn punctuated his words.

"We have not discussed the Brotherhood since Ansidrion first joined, a week ago."

"No, we have not," he agreed.

"I am surprised that Ansidrion has taken such bold action," I admitted.

"Oh? Yes, I am as well." Yhako shrugged. "But what causes your surprise?"

"Because I had always thought of him as slothful!" I laughed. "He has never seemed to me the sort of man who might take direct action to solve a problem, even when he so fully believes in the solution."

"Slothful?" Yhako pursed his lips. "I do not suppose I had ever thought of him in such terms."

"Not ever? But think of how he sleeps half his days away. Look at how he lives his life: either sleeping or in his studies. I understand that the two of you have arranged it as such, but a man who spends so many hours in his bed and the other half of his day at his desk is the kind that will have many hours for thought but nary a minute for action."

"No, Fe'n. It is not this way at all. Ansidrion has not behaved in this manner out of sloth, but rather from pride. He sees himself as a prophet who has yet to reveal his prophecy. He believes that he will one day discover a great truth unto which many men will be drawn. He believes he is capable of everything that bespeaks glory. I cannot even begin to explain how intensely he was drawn to Maddith's *Miracles* when he first read of them. Every day it was a new revelation from him: 'Yhako, I shall recreate this miracle,' or 'I believe I know of several miracles that Maddith has forgotten entirely.'" He donned a distant smile, thinking fondly of his youth with his brother. "Recall how doubtfully he responded when you spoke of your Pelatt?"

"He absolutely refused to consider that Pelatt might be the Noble Laborer," I remembered. "But then how can he take such interest in *The Miracles*?"

"He does not doubt *The Miracles*, or the Noble Laborer, or you. He merely could not entertain the idea that you had revealed this miracle, for if your Pelatt had been the Noble Laborer, that would mean that he might never find his own. You did not intend it, of course, and I doubt Ansidrion even realized it immediately, but you alienated that miracle from him."

Ansidrion had a rigid determination to be correct at the cost of everything else, but I had always thought it was because of conviction in his education. I did not consider that it was deeper, that it got to what he saw as his life's purpose. But if he were so determined to be a revealer of truth, it seemed very contrary to the concept of reform, for how could he be open to anything other than his own ideas? But I declined to say this at that moment. Instead, I returned to the original topic. "Then how has this led him to the Ilepyan Brotherhood?"

Yhako did not respond to this query directly, but instead went far astray. "Federan, I wish you could have known Sirlat. She was truly a great woman, and you might understand our history and cause with much greater significance had she been able to lead you."

"But I have known of Sirlat through her words. She has sent me many letters, and although I neglected to read them at the time, I have since reviewed many of them, and gleaned great knowledge from them."

"But Sirlat were words least of all. She was a woman of action, of leadership. I am not surprised that she would have been seen as a leader of the revolution in Yafia, as a woman even worthy of assassination by that evil bishop. I have met no person as adept as she at finding the proper solution in any situation, and bringing it about without hesitation or flaw."

"Then we need someone like her here in Ilepya now, do we not?"

"Precisely. Sirlat is exactly what we need in this time and place. Ansidrion has realized it, as well, and he now seeks to *be* Sirlat. He has been a man of letters long enough; now he feels that his prophecy will come in the form of deed."

"And do you believe it? Can Ansidrion become Sirlat?"

"I do not know, Federan. Ansidrion has never been a man of deed. He has never truly sought to put his learning to use. The Ilepyan Brotherhood will be the first test thereof. His likeliest downfall is that he will feel entitled to leadership, and I worry that this might prevent him from doing the most good he possibly can."

"But that is how we all are, I suppose. When we first try anything, we must have our way at it, and must learn through our failures as we go."

Yhako nodded and we were silent for a moment.

"But if Sirlat was a person of action whom Ansidrion seeks to emulate, and our sister Qhema has clearly taken her own action, then what of you and me? Should we not take action as well?"

Yhako grinned. "There is still the priesthood for you, is there not? Or has that since changed?"

I smiled and shook my head to acknowledge the jest.

But then he sighed. "I am not a leader like Sirlat; Grontinion is not for me. I am not adventurous like Qhema; Vend is not for me. I am not bold like Ansidrion; the Ilepyan Brotherhood is not for me. None of it seems to fit me very well. But you will find yours yet."

Yhako seemed wistful, vulnerable for the first time ever I had seen. It made me uncomfortable, and I immediately sought to argue. "As shall you, Yhako! None of those things is right for me, either. Each of us shall find his path."

"No, I am becoming an old man now, and the time for me to make my way in this world has come and passed. I shall be a scholar, a man who studies letters and shares his insights with others."

"Old man? Nonsense! You are but a year older than Ansidrion, who is only now making his way with the Ilepyan Brotherhood. You still have many years ahead of you, and besides, you might be able to achieve amazing things in very little time."

"Unless this is enough for me. Perhaps to be a man of letters is all I want. I am quite accomplished at it, after all."

"Indeed, you are the wisest man I have ever met, Yhako, and I doubt there is a scholar as talented as you in this entire country. But this talent is one that you should share with the world, one through which you can bring about great things."

"And I have already begun to, for if you will permit me, I would like to claim a bit of credit for you. You will do remarkable things, I know, and I suppose one must acclaim your elder brother who, in your youth, constantly harassed you until you changed your course."

He smiled and I did the same, but I did not feel joy. He spoke almost as a man on his deathbed might speak to his son, and it seemed to lack hope entirely. I had always thought of Yhako as a man concerned with the future where Ansidrion was far too contained in the present. But if an eye to the future produced such a melancholy outlook, perhaps there was no reason for optimism. "I shall grant you claim for me, of course, but you must know that you will do greater things than change my feeble mind, brother."

"I see no such thing greater than that." And then he stood and left the room, patting my shoulder as he passed by. He had given me a new perspective on Ansidrion, but now I worried for him, Yhako, as he seemed to be a man without hope. I knew he was capable of more if he could alter his path just as Ansidrion had, but at the very least, I could give him courage by achieving the greatness he had come to expect in me.

When I lay in bed that evening, I began by thinking more about Yhako and the hope he lacked, but I soon found that my thoughts drifted toward Pelatt, my Noble Laborer. This was not an entirely strange sensation; he often crossed my mind. Every time I left the house I yearned to encounter his smile in the streets, but when I did see him it was unwelcome, for he only came when I closed my eyes and I heard him scream in pain. I thought about Pelatt and Ma't and that fateful day, but I had also grown fond of imagining what his life was like. I fantasized that he had once worked in the timber yards outside of the city, and that he had many sisters who adored him, and that he looked after his mother in her advancing age. I believed that now, following his injuries, he spent his days in bed, and had to be cared for by his doting sisters, and that his body yearned to labor as it had always done. Perhaps none of it had been true, but Pelatt had been among the few people I had ever met in my life, and I felt at all moments that I knew and loved everything about him, despite knowing almost no details of his upbringing and lifestyle.

Those were all idle thoughts of Pelatt the man, as he was in my head. But this night in particular, I thought of Pelatt as the Noble Laborer, as the straightforward, honest man of simple and pure character. In his simplicity, the Noble Laborer never wavered nor hesitated. His decisions were not complicated by nuance, but rather were made entirely by instinct. That night I felt that Yhako's inaction was perhaps because he was too intelligent. Yhako could conceive of anything. He could think of any reason why any action might be unwise, so he often ended up doing nothing at all. If only all of the complications could be pared away. If only he could be simpler, and could believe in and pursue simple things.

In many ways Ansidrion followed this path. He was capable of conceiving the nuance and complication, but once conceived, he often discarded it entirely. For Ansidrion everything was absolute; if it was wrong, it was evil and horrible and false. If he took action, he pursued that action with all of his heart, and let nothing and no one put him off of it. I did not wish Yhako to be as brash as Ansidrion, but he could afford more of the Noble Laborer's simplicity.

The next morning, Yhako required to meet with other merchants for the *as'shelik* business, so he was out of the house as soon as the sun had risen. It was rare, in those days, for me to have a moment alone with Ansidrion, as Yhako was in the home at nearly all times. We took breakfast together, and although I remained apprehensive about the work the Brotherhood did, I had also developed a stifling curiosity of the revolution they intended. "What does your Brotherhood plan?" I asked. "When you give them your night, what comes of it?"

Ansidrion seemed to glow at the mere mention of the Brotherhood. "Well, *dofit*, just this night previous we found ourselves planning the *evatarr*." He paused, waiting for me to ask what this term meant. I merely shrugged, so he continued. "The *evatarr* comes from the Gringellic term *ewitterada*, which, along with the *tarbhasht*, or labor strike, was perhaps the most important weapon of the Yiffen revolution. It is a commercial action, in which a person avoids giving his business to those who oppose him."

"Oppose him?" I asked. "Oppose him how?"

"By holding opposing political views, of course. The supporters of the Yiffen revolution avoided buying products from known supporters of the existing tyrannical government."

"I suppose this provides more resources for revolutionaries, while preventing them from falling into the hands of the oppressors?"

"Precisely that," Ansidrion said, nodding. "And when the guilds of Grontinion and Rakka held all of the governing power in their hands, at the height of the revolution, the financial incentives of siding with the revolutionaries proved decisive. The larger guilds supported the revolution, while those that did not faced an *ewitterada* so harsh that they collapsed, and were eventually overrun by pro-revolutionary guild members."

"But our guilds are nowhere near as strong. Most businesses in Ilepya are not even organized into guilds; how can an *evatarr* accomplish anything here?"

"We do not need guilds, Federan. We shall merely compile a list of the families who have acted against us, and instruct our friends to avoid their businesses. This list will even reach our allies abroad, and the people of Colof and Yafia will not trade with them either."

"It does sound like quite a burden for our opponents. Perhaps some of their businesses might be ruined, while others might be convinced to withdraw their support from the government." We were silent for a moment, as Ansidrion nodded with pride. Then I discovered the flaw. "But what if we can find no alternative to our opponents?"

Ansidrion frowned at me. "What is this? What do you mean?"

"What if every known family in a certain business opposes us? The Bishop has close ties with the Dolith family, and they produce all of the red beans in this part of the country. Shall we no longer eat them?"

"Of course we shall not!"

"And what if we were to discover that every tailor from here to Pondital supported the government against us?"

"Then we would learn to sew our own clothing."

I shook my head. "I am not sure if you will convince many people to abandon their accustomed trades."

"It is not unreasonable to ask that people temporarily surrender a few luxuries for a cause as important as this." Ansidrion scoffed. "It is but a small sacrifice. Perhaps you will buy your bread from the enemy, but I know not where you will find your cash, as not a *dorvdiyar* from Father's business will fall into their hands."

"Ansidrion, this is not what I intend. Of course I shall comply with it. It is merely that—"

"That you do not believe in it."

"But if you say it has worked before, so I shall trust you that it will work again, and I wish you the best of luck in it," I said, attempting to recover his good will."

"Good," he said brusquely, ripping a loaf of bread in two.

The morning had only just begun and I had already alienated him. We would have another hour or two together, and I wanted to make the best of the time. We had not had a particularly strong relationship over the last decade, but there was reason to rectify that, and I had seen this morning as the perfect opportunity. "I had not meant to challenge you, I merely wanted to understand. There are many things that you understand better than I, after all." Flattery did not seem to have its desired effect; he gnawed on his bread, and his forehead remained furrowed. "Yhako, for one, is a subject I should leave up to you to explain. Do you believe he is content with his studies alone?"

Ansidrion continued chewing. Then, after a moment, he swallowed and raised his eyebrows. "You mean to say his studies and his business?"

"Yes, I suppose I do. Is he content with this, what he has, forever? I know that I desire to do greater things in my life, and you have already begun to undertake your own by way of the Brotherhood. Shall Yhako accomplish nothing more than reading and writing?"

Ansidrion sighed. "I believe he wants nothing more. Yhako has always seen himself as a prophet." At this I smiled, recalling Yhako's words about Ansidrion's desired prophecy just the evening before. "He believes that he will achieve his most important accomplishments through his letters. He is full of wisdom, as you know, and he believes that all he must do to change the world is to find the proper way of letting it out. Leave actions for others, he feels, for everyone is capable of action, but only a select few are capable of word."

"Do you believe as much? Will he be satisfied in the end? Will he accomplish anything?"

"Federan, I wish you could have known Sirlat." Was I dreaming? This seemed to be the exact conversation I had had the previous evening, merely with my brothers switched. "Yes, you know her through her letters, but she was much more than that. She was a brilliant person; a woman who could form an argument faster than you could pose your question. Yhako and I were in awe of her in our youth, and even now you see the shadow she casts over us. She is a hero in a foreign land, and will probably soon be thought of as a hero here. She has already accomplished all she ever can in life, and yet she has done more than I think I might ever do."

"Should that not inspire Yhako to do more with himself? If Sirlat is his hero, should he not attempt to accomplish all Sirlat had?"

"But firstly, Sirlat was always a student. She loved reading, and as you have seen, she was a prolific writer. Her singular quest in life was the search of knowledge, and so Yhako has decided to pursue the same."

"Yet Yhako has not found himself speaking out for his cause, as Sirlat had. Yhako merely pursues knowledge for its own end; he has not used it for the greater good."

"And that is his decision, Federan," Ansidrion snapped. "If Yhako determines that he should take an action, we must leave it to Yhako to take that action. You have questioned my decision to join the Ilepyan Brotherhood, yet you also begrudge Yhako for not doing likewise. And what have you done?"

"I do not begrudge him, I merely wonder if it is enough for his own contentment." I ignored Ansidrion's question because I knew it was correct and I did not want to face it. I had done nothing more than Yhako. But I did not know what to do! If the Ilepyan Brotherhood was the only option, then action was not right for me. Knowing that I could not address this accusation, and not wanting to be pressed on it further, I quickly retreated to the study. When Ansidrion followed, several minutes later, we said nothing, and remained silent until Yhako arrived the next hour.

Soon, we found that our lives revolved around the Ilepyan Brotherhood. Even when no one spoke of it—and, indeed, Yhako and I mentioned it very rarely—it was clearly a thought on all of our minds. By not speaking it, we were focused on it even more, expending all of our energy on avoiding it. That seemed to give it more gravity, and I think even Ansidrion knew that it was the primary subject of our lives now.

Just as we had the second week, Yhako and I continued to sit down to converse after Ansidrion left for his meetings. I believe we both needed it, as it allowed us to speak our concerns in as frank a manner as possible. Sometimes the Brotherhood was only on the periphery of the conversation, but even so, Ansidrion was much of all we were able to talk about.

"I was never much of a brother to Ansidrion, I am sure you know," Yhako suggested to me as we spoke one day.

"No, not at all. The two of you always seemed to be a united force, and I felt that if one of you held an opinion, the other would as well, although he might present it with more aggression, and you with more wile."

"That is true. Ansidrion and I are frequently in agreement, and we hold many of the same values. But I was never quite able to give him what he needed from me. When Sirlat was in the home, the two of them were always together, and Ansidrion saw her as a hero. I might have felt the same way, but that I resented it; Ansidrion and I were so near in age that I expected to be his mentor. But instead, I was like Father, always full of ideas, always lost in thought. When he became old enough to think for himself, Ansidrion loved to passionately debate with Sirlat, becoming fiery in his convictions. Sirlat always won the debates, of course, and although Ansidrion would never concede, he could be heard to hold the same position as Sirlat several days later. I, meanwhile, listened to it all, but said very little.

"After Sirlat left, Ansidrion was devastated, and this was accelerated by Father's death and Mother's sudden change. He and I both felt we had no one, but while this was no great loss for me, Ansidrion was adrift, and needed someone upon whom he could depend. So I had to step in and become his mentor, but I was fumbling at it, and often preferred to withdraw from him than to help him grow. I loved that he looked to me for ideas, but I hated that he challenged me, and that he demanded my attention so frequently.

"When we left Mother and you in Kapabaj, the relationship became more strained than ever, because we had no common enemy, no one against whom we were united. I loved him, and I admired him and on my best days I enjoyed laboring and studying at his side, but other times I felt that there was no reason for the two of us to even so much as live together."

"I had never suspected as much," I interjected. "I did not sense that the two of you might feel anything but love toward one another."

"I am glad for that, because I hoped that neither he nor you would ever notice. This was my struggle, and although it involved others, I felt that it was purely internal. I knew that I had a responsibility to him as my brother, but I also felt that a common belief system and bloodline alone are not enough to keep two men together. I grew miserable; exhausted in both body and mind, because of the great toll this conflict exacted from me. I still slept at night during those times, but I was never fully rested with Ansidrion around, for I was forced to spend every waking moment with him, to devote all of my conscious energy to his well-being. Ansidrion, as you know, lives outside of his head, and relies on validation from those around him to thrive. He demanded it from me constantly, and I never had time to myself."

"It is odd for you to say such a thing, for I felt the opposite. When Ansidrion came to visit me in Kapabaj in those days, I felt joy, for unlike with Mother, I always knew his mind exactly, and had a constant source of interaction. He doted upon me, spent his every minute talking to me or seeking to entertain me."

"That is precisely what saved us. You needed attention from someone more stable than Mother, especially after Qhema left, and he was just the man to give it to you. I convinced him that he should visit you on occasion, but this was due to my own selfish motives, as I merely wanted a week or two apart from him. He would return to find me refreshed, emotionally equipped to handle his codependence. He never acknowledged it, but I think some part of him realized that, whenever he returned home from Kapabaj, I was always more pleasant to him, and for that reason he enjoyed it all the more.

"Eventually, though, even these small respites were not enough. I would grow accustomed to his presence once again, and become exhausted. My productivity in studying or toiling at the business receded anew, and I despaired of ever being able to labor successfully with him around. Knowing that I had to spend time away from him, but that I could never say it, I devised a plan. I knew that Ansidrion had never taken much interest in the *as'shelik*, but that he thoroughly enjoyed his studies. I needed to be able to undertake both, and I enjoyed both besides, so I proposed to him that I should take on all of the business responsibilities. I had to find a way to spend this time alone, so in return, Ansidrion would take on all of the sleeping responsibilities."

"Now the story! I have always been so curious about this arrangement, especially why you would agree to it. Now that I know the details, I wonder why Ansidrion did not suspect you had fooled him."

"You know how impetuous Ansidrion is. When he is given favorable terms, he never thinks to question the motives. I had offered him the things he wanted most in the world. And so, without a second thought, he took it. He took it with a great grin on his face as though he had won a glorious battle and, indeed, perhaps he had. It is entirely possible that such a thing were his plan all along, and were you to talk to him, he would tell you that he fooled me into this agreement.

"I had thought that adjusting to this new lifestyle would be gravely difficult. I had been sleeping all my life—or, a few hours of each night of my life—and to forego it entirely was a remarkable change. But the truth was that I had been living without rest for years. Being constantly at Ansidrion's side had worn me down such that even sleep exhausted me. He found his way into my dreams, troubling me with his bold pronouncements and heavy arguments as I sought rest. Now, as I had each night to myself, it was more restorative than any of that shallow sleep could ever have been. I felt *more* rested with the change. And, what was more, I found spending time with Ansidrion enjoyable. Studying at his side was a pleasure, and we no longer competed with one another, but rather complemented each other."

"And your relationship has been ideal ever since?"

"As near to ideal as can be with a pair of men as different as the two of us. He does things that I would not, and I am sure he finds many of my actions confusing, but I have learned to accept him as I never had in our youth."

"I had no idea that you were so intolerant of others!" I smiled at him, surprised at the depth of his revelations. I had never thought of Ansidrion as so dependent, or of Yhako as so solitary. "Had you felt this way about me, as well?"

"Oh no, not you, Federan. You were much easier to manage. You were such a quiet child that if I were not careful, I would not have noticed you at all. I do not mean this as a slight, for this is a characteristic I enjoy in a person. No, you were much more like me; quietly curious and thoughtful, saying much less than you could have. I enjoyed you, although I am sure it never seemed that way."

"No, that is correct. You did not think much of me in those days. Although I thought very little of you either."

"And for that I apologize. In my youth I was so concerned with my own thoughts that I had no time for others. I did not know how to converse with someone so much younger than I, as I had spent much of my childhood with siblings of my own age, with Father, or alone. Besides, Ansidrion required so much of my attention that I could not make much time for you."

I suddenly felt that Yhako and I were alike, much more than I had ever realized. He had always been an admirable but distant figure, a man of few words who kept many hours to himself. I had not had the chance to know him much as a person, and having this conversation with him now made me happy. It seemed right that I should tell him as much. "It would appear, then, that Mother, Sirlat, and Ansidrion are cut from the same cloth, as are Father, you, and I." I smiled at him.

To my surprise, however, he did not smile back, but rather looked vulnerably nostalgic once again. "Yes, it was so," he said. I felt as if he had intended to go on, but he stopped short. Yet, in a peculiar way, I knew exactly what he meant to say, and I, too, wanted him not to say it. This statement, completely unsaid and even unprecedented in the current conversation, loomed over us. It demanded to be uttered, so Yhako and I both knew we could say nothing else, lest it take control and transform our words into it.

Mother, Sirlat, and Ansidrion were alike. Those three had made sacrifices, taken daring decisions for their beliefs, risking everything to do what they thought was right. For Mother, it had cost her her sanity. For Sirlat it had cost her her life. And yet, here sat Yhako and I, doing nothing for our beliefs, simply spouting our truths from the comforts of our luxurious home. Yhako had already lost hope of doing anything. He had already accepted that he would die like Father, having accumulated an impressive wealth of knowledge, but having used none of it to make a difference in the world around him.

It was at that moment that I vowed not to be like Yhako. We might have been born with some of the same characteristics, but I could not allow myself to give in to this cowardice. Father had imparted his wisdom unto Yhako, and Yhako his unto me, but now I would do something with it. I did not quite know what yet, only that it had to be something important, and it had to be soon.

The next morning, Ansidrion excitedly described what he had learned the night before. After four weeks, this had become routine, but this time Ansidrion truly had news. "The Dictator of Hihaythea will come to Ilepya in the next month. He has already left the capital, Poonlon, and he passes along the coast this very moment."

"When has the Dictator most recently come to Ilepya?" I asked. "I cannot remember him ever coming to our city."

"It has been many years," Yhako agreed.

"Nine, say the Brothers," Ansidrion reported.

"Nine years? The second largest city in all of Hihaythea, and he has not visited it in nine years?" I was stunned.

"You know that is not unusual, Federan," Yhako reminded me. "The entire government consists of natives of Poonlon, who give Ilepya nary a thought. Now Ansidrion, what does the Brotherhood mean to do with this information? Shall you attempt to keep him away?"

"No, Yhako, we welcome him! Let him come to Ilepya!"

His tone made me nervous. "Why? What sort of embarrassment do you have planned for him here?"

"No embarrassment, Federan. No shame at all! Because I happen to know that once the Dictator sets foot in Ilepya, he will never leave!"

Yhako's eyes widened and his mouth drew tight. He glared at Ansidrion. "Will you kill him?" He whispered.

"Shall I? I do not know if I shall. But someone will, yes."

"How? How can you succeed at it?"

"It is not decided yet. But the Brotherhood will not allow the Dictator to come to us without we demonstrate our power, nor without he pay for his oppression."

I was horrified. "What will killing him accomplish? You know murder to be wrong! How can you celebrate in planning the death of a man?"

"Federan, this is what they do. They have been killing innocent people for years—they have done it with Sirlat. The only way they can be stopped is by removing those who command these killings."

"They have done it with Sirlat, yes. Bishop Irat had Sirlat assassinated, and look at what it did for Irat! He is dead now, and everything he had believed in is wiped away. Is this what you want for yourself?"

Ansidrion shook his head. "Federan, it is not so simple. The government must be stopped, and little labor strikes and angry letters will not achieve it. We need something bigger."

I was so enraged that I could not even tolerate speaking with him. Instead, I stood up and walked out, throwing myself upon my bed in anger. "Yes, you wish to be a leader, to be a prophet, a man of bold action," I shouted as I stormed off. "But is murder the sort of bold action you want to be responsible for? What kind of leader plots to kill a man?" I had vowed not to be like Yhako, but I could not be like Ansidrion, either. If this were a revolution predicated on violence, I could take no part in it.

Yhako and Ansidrion let me have the day to myself, perhaps preoccupied in their own argument. I expected that Yhako might disagree with Ansidrion's actions, but probably accepted them immediately. They might have discussed the issue as I lay in my bed; perhaps Yhako was attempting to dissuade him. But I had learned from Yhako already that there could be no stopping Ansidrion. This he meant to do, and he would let nothing prevent him.

I needed to speak with someone about this, as my frustration with Ansidrion's choices caused too much angst within my head. But Yhako and Ansidrion were the only people I trusted, and I could not speak with either of them on the subject any more. Whom else did I have?

Suddenly, I remembered Qhema. Of course, I had another sibling, whom I once adored! I had not seen her in many years, but perhaps I could write her a letter, in the hope that I might one day have a means to have it delivered.

I set about writing, beginning with a brief apology that I had not written more, and then leaping into an account of the assassination plan. It weighed heavily on my mind, and I knew that I could not distract myself with other ideas before I talked through this crisis. But after a brief description of it, and then a comparison of it to Sirlat's own assassination, I moved on. Writing to Qhema, imagining a conversation with her, made me feel like a child again, speaking with my long-absent guardian. I wanted to tell her everything—every foolish little thought and adventure—that I had in my head: from the Noble Laborer to the fantastic stew that Ansidrion had served the previous week. By the time night began to fall, I had written three pages, and was preparing another sheet.

But then I heard strange sounds outside of my window. They were people's voices, but there were more of them than I would have expected for our quiet street, and they sounded angry. I opened my window and led my head out of it, but I could only see a few shadows pass by, tucked away into the alley as I was. So I stuffed the letter into my pocket, grabbed my coat, and stepped outside. It was rather foolish of me to run heedlessly into the streets during those times of growing tension, but I felt inexorably drawn to this noise, like Ansidrion to the Brotherhood.

There, on the street, was a group of about a dozen people, walking together. Under the cover of darkness, they shouted phrases in unison. *"Peilav kelgarim*—the people demand liberty." *"Yhahram alu*—the light is with me."* By the time I stepped onto Trafgha Street, they had nearly rounded the corner out of view, as they walked quickly, with their bodies pressed close together. From a distance, after they had left the street, I heard them call *"tarbhasht.*" Was this a reformist protest? Were they encouraging their neighbors to strike?

I hastened back inside and went directly to Ansidrion's chamber. We had not spoken since our argument that morning, and I certainly had not accepted his new course, but I had to know what he knew about this protest. To my surprise, he was not asleep, but rather was writing at his small table.

"Ansidrion, heard you those people on the street?"

"No, I have heard nothing. What people?"

"Just this moment, there were a dozen men and women walking the street together, shouting about the *tarbhasht*. I believe it was a protest."

"A protest? Here, on Trafgha Street?"

"Yes, right here, although they quickly proceeded toward the center of town. Is this the Brotherhood's doing?"

"No, we do not protest. We have planned no *tarbhasht*."

"Could there be one that you do not know about? They shouted those words as clearly as ever I have heard them."

"No, I know of all of the Brotherhood's doing. No protest, no *tarbhasht*."

"Then this was a protest arranged by some other group. There must be others organizing against the government!"

"I suppose, although a protest will not achieve much. They will meet their end at the hands of the *asdesaj*. No, this is not the Brotherhood's doing, for we would not use such base tactics."

Ansidrion's smug and dismissive attitude disinterested me, so I left abruptly and returned to my room. Others were taking action as well. There was a way to take part in the revolution without joining the Brotherhood. Of course, this method might have been even more perilous, but seeing people appear in the streets, in complete defiance of their bishop and his police, inspired me. Their mere presence showed a refusal to fear, which was the ultimate anti-government action. I knew very little of their motive or history, but merely from a few seconds of observation, I felt a sense of deep admiration.

I thought about their phrase, *yhahram alu*. I did not quite understand what it meant, but the sound of it appealed to me. I lay down in bed and turned it over in my head a few times, thinking of what the light might represent, falling asleep with the mysterious words echoing in my ears.

The next morning, I asked Yhako about the protests, and he said that he knew nothing of them, either. But I was determined to find out more.

I took my first steps out into the streets that evening. Ansidrion, as I learned the night before, had no interest in it. Besides, with the preparations for the visit of the Dictator, he was now meeting with the Brotherhood several nights a week. Yhako also declined to join me, as he saw little purpose in street demonstrations. "What will you say by it?" He asked. "Making your presence known will do little, for it is clear that the authorities know that some among us demand reform, but they mean to give us nothing."

"It is to demonstrate that we are free. By appearing in the streets in a protest that is known to be part of the reform, we are confirming to the Bishop and his servants that we do not fear them. We are showing our dissent to the Bishop, so that he knows that we mean to speak our minds."

"You will speak and you will be heard," he said. "But your voices will do nothing more than draw the Bishop's bloody will to you. There are hardly enough people who take to the streets to make a difference."

I had never heard such cynicism from Yhako. "But there are hundreds of other people who agree with our cause but are afraid to be heard. By us showing our willingness to demonstrate, they will be inspired to show theirs. Forty people cannot topple a government, but forty can inspire a hundred, who can inspire a thousand, who can inspire a million. And if a million people willed it, do not doubt that they could turn over even the heaviest boulder."

"Your cause and feeling is noble, Fe'n, but I do not believe it is the best." He sighed. "I fear for your safety as you do this, and I wish you would not."

"And I feel the same way about Ansidrion. I know that I must do something, but I cannot take the action Ansidrion has. Perhaps you can do something that will worry Ansidrion, and we shall be equal." I smiled.

Yhako returned the smile and embraced me. "Have care," he told me. "Be cautious in your risk."

I nodded, and then grabbed my coat and stepped into the evening.

I made my way carefully toward the center of town, where I imagined the protests to be, darting around corners and pausing frequently to listen or look for signs of the *asdesaj*. The hour was not as late as it had been when I heard the protesters the previous night, so there was no action on Trafgha Street. When I arrived at Malqhom Street, I was among the first ten, and I initially stood off from the others, not knowing what to do or how to interact with them. Malqhom Street carried special meaning for me, as it bore my father's name. What would Father think of his posthumous son joining such a protest? In that moment, I wished that there were a Fulviya Street, so that we could protest along it and show Mother what I had become.

Then, just as we were approaching Pariatt Street, the people before me clustered together and shouted *"yhahram alu!"* The sudden cry startled me, and I jumped at the sound of it. At they noticed me, and more pointedly, noticed that I had not taken part in their proclamation. "What brings you here, young man?" One of them called out to me, her voice hushed but urgent. *"Desaj?"* She posed the question in a whisper to his fellows.

"No!" I answered quickly. They were on watch for the police, of course, and the last thing I wanted them to think was that I was part of the police force. "I have merely come to join your protest, but this is my first night, and I have not yet learned of your methods."

At this the woman who first spoke to me approached, while the others continued forward toward Pariatt Street. "Welcome, young man," she said to me. "We are glad to see you in the streets, but we are always wary that the *asdesaj* have come to infiltrate us and learn our ways."

"I am not *desaj*, madam," I repeated. How would I prove it to her? I thought of mentioning the Ilepyan Brotherhood, but protester though she was, she was also a stranger, and I did not want to further spread word of Ansidrion's illegal scheming. "I am Fe'n, of the Ponyhubiresh family," I told her. "My sister Sirlat was murdered by Bishop Irat in Grontinion a few years previous, and my brothers are active here in the reformist ideology."

"I suppose you do not have the accent that all of the *asdesaj* seem to have," she said, looking me over. "Come, you will be welcome among us. My name is Yhonam."

"It is my pleasure to meet you. And what should I know as we begin, Yhonam? What caused the group of you to shout?"

"We began because there were thirteen of us. That is the number we have set—our minimum, I suppose. Any fewer than that and we feign merely to be lovers coming home from an evening tryst. The *asdesaj* travel in groups of no more than six. If we are thirteen, there is enough for us to unite against them should they attack, and still have another person free to seek further assistance. Thus, when we are thirteen, we are emboldened to begin to protest."

"Very well, that is simple enough." I did not understand how they expected anyone observing from a distance for a night not to learn this strategy. But I was in no place to question a movement I had only just joined, so I kept silent.

"Every evening, as the sun sets, we leave our homes and begin toward the center of the city. We keep to certain paths so that our numbers accumulate faster, making us safer. You seem to have known it already; from this part of the city we find Malqhom as quickly as possible, and then spend our time moving between Pariatt, Tajarr, and Turka Streets."

"That is sensible, but why do you not go to the true center of town: Maidia Street?"

"No, we shall never go to Maidia Street." She grabbed my arm and led me in the direction that the others had gone. "It is along Maidia Street, at the Apgha Palace, where the *asdesaj* are, and if we go there, they shall bring all of their force against us. Were we to go to the Apgha, the government would feel threatened by our power, and would surely destroy us. By protesting along the other streets, we merely call the neighbors to action and embarrass the government, but they do not know how to respond."

It seemed relatively wise, and yet, it also felt too cautious. "But if the government is not threatened by us, how will we accomplish anything?" By this time we had rounded a corner and were approaching a group of twenty or more protesters.

"Do you believe a group of women and men this small could threaten our government, which is protected by the *asdesaj*? No, they could do away with us immediately. We must wait until we are large enough, which is perhaps many more days yet."

"But you seem to have grown fast enough. I have not seen a single protest in these streets until the previous night. How has this begun? Why suddenly are there so many Ilepyans in the streets, where before there were none?"

"There was a raid on the timber yards," Yhonam explained. "We do not know why it happened—the *asdesaj* appeared and attacked the workers, injuring or killing several of the people who labored there."

I gasped. I thought about Pelatt as the subject of an attack he could not have expected, and did not deserve. "It must have come from the Bishop. No one else could have ordered such an attack."

"I suppose so," she agreed. "It was completely arbitrary. We had no way of knowing it would come. And from it, the protests have begun spontaneously. The timberers who escaped the attack fled into the streets of the city, near Solom Street, and began shouting. The neighbors heard cries about violence at the hands of the *asdesaj*, and because many of the residents in that area have connections to the timberers, they were sympathetic, and they joined the timberers in the streets. Since that day, two weeks ago, the protests have grown larger and crept east, until they have arrived at this part of town last night."

If the protests had gone on for two weeks, Yhako or Ansidrion or both would likely have known about them, but had declined to tell me, perhaps knowing how I might be lured to them. I might have felt resentment had I not been so drawn in. "Did you labor in the timber yards, madam?" I asked. Perhaps she knew Pelatt!

"No, but my cousin, Danor, does. Or he did until this week."

"My apologies. Was he hurt in the raid?"

"No. But the timberers have ceased to work. They do so to protest the actions of the *asdesaj*, as the government makes money from the timber yards, which it then uses to pay the *asdesaj* to attack the workers."

"It is a *tarbhasht*," I said.

"Indeed it is. Let our labor not be used as a means to harm us."

The people had awoken exactly as Yhako and Ansidrion had wanted. "So how will your cousin survive? How can the timberers live without their wages?"

"I do not know. They do not know. But it must be done."

I thought about my own Noble Laborer, somewhere on the streets, going some days without food, some nights without shelter. It was not right that such good people lived with so little and did so much, while my brothers and I lived in luxury and spent our days at our leisure. "Tell me, madam, will you see your cousin soon? Here, take this to him," I said, retrieving a few *bavdiyar* coins from my pocket and pressing them into her hand. "And should you need it, you may take some for yourself."

The woman shook her head. "No, I cannot accept this from you."

"You must," I insisted. "And if you exhaust this, return to my house, on Trafgha Street, and I shall give you more, for we have plenty."

"I need nothing, sir, for I continue to labor. But my cousin will do well with this. Thank you, Mister Ponyhubiresh! We are forever in your debt."

"Your debt is already forgiven, as the risks that he and you have taken for the greater good are payment enough. And please, should you know anyone else in need, give them my name and tell them to come to my home."

The woman gave no response, and her eyes did not again meet mine. Instead, we continued on in silence.

When we arrived at the place where Eparam and Pariatt Streets met, there were perhaps one hundred people or more already there, come to protest against the government. I heard more of the chants, and *yhahram alu* resonated through my mind once again. The shouts were not at full volume—we were about a half mile from Maidia Street, and perhaps less than a mile from the Apgha. Even with a hundred of us, we stood no chance against the government. Instead, the present goal was to bring others to attention: a literal awakening from the Ilepyan slumber. Our neighbors were asleep in their homes, content with their current lives, ignorant to how much better life could be. We, the timberers and their allies, meant to tell people about the liberty they lacked, and make them join us in the street.

As it happened, this intersection was but a three minute walk away from the temple on Eparam Street, where I had visited Ma't so many times. At this hour, Ma't likely slept in his bedchamber adjoining the temple, but I wished he might choose this time to go for a walk. If he could see me now he would be horrified at what I had become. If I were to see him, I did not know what I would do.

Yhonam placed her hand upon my back and then disappeared into the crowd, saying *yhahram alu* as she walked amongst the others. I repeated the phrase. Thereafter I was alone amongst the timberers for the night. We stood and shouted, and walked along Pariatt Street between Eparam and Turka. At some hours there would be reports of *asdesaj* coming, and we would dart down little alleyways, but I never saw them for myself. Either the reports were false, or the *asdesaj* were too small in numbers to attack us.

Several times, people leaned out of their window and shouted at us to be quiet and return home. These moments were disheartening initially, but then I saw my first conversion. A few of us had spilled over onto Iromal Street and were chanting our phrases, when a young woman opened her window and glared at us. Then, after a moment, she shuttered her window once again, and appeared at her front door. I expected her to scold us, but instead she approached one of the other protesters—a large, gruff-looking man with a grey beard—and asked what we did that night.

"We call attention to the injustices of the government," the great timberer responded. "They have attacked the timberers without reason, so now we mean to tell everyone. You are not safe from the *asdesaj* if we are not."

"Then what shall we do about it?" I heard the neighbor ask.

"Come," said the timberer. "Join us in the streets this night. Let us show that we will not tolerate it."

The pair of them merged into the crowd and the night marched on. If the protests could call me to action, if they could so easily summon this young woman to join them, then many hundreds more in Ilepya were waiting to be awakened as well. I shouted *yhahram alu* into the night, and continued protesting with renewed enthusiasm. I was not a gregarious young man, so I did not speak much with my fellows, but when a faint orange light began to emerge from the distant sea, I noticed that the crowds along Pariatt Street had thinned, and many of the people began to disperse southward.

"Do we not protest into the morning?" I asked one of the timberers.

"We do not. It is not safe to protest during the daylight, for there are many more people out, including more *asdesaj*. Our faces are easier to see, and some of the neighbors walking the streets, who might be opposed to our cause, can easily identify us and give our names to the bishop. No, you must go home now, as we all do, lest you put yourself in more danger."

"Yes sir, thank you." Few people in this town were capable of identifying me, as I had kept almost entirely to myself throughout my life. But my earlier courage dissipated as I thought about how much power Ma't, the one man who could recognize me, had. I agreed that it was best to avoid any more danger for the time.

I felt that I should be exhausted, but I was not. I had been on my feet, shouting, walking, running for the entire night. The sun arose and I felt invigorated. I strolled down Trafgha Street and stepped foot into the house to find Yhako in the kitchen, preparing a bit of food for the three of us.

"*Dofit*, here you are! Safe and healthy, I see." He smiled at me.

"Yes, brother I have had quite a night. The streets are full of joy, of action, and I cannot wait to return tomorrow night, and every night thereafter until we have brought about the change we demand."

Yhako looked a bit crestfallen. "Then it was pleasing to you? I suppose I cannot put you off of this danger."

"I am as obstinate as Ansidrion and his Brotherhood. I have found my purpose, my way to our cause."

"Yes, well in speaking of Ansidrion, he is not arrived yet. I expect him any minute, but between the worry the two of you provoke in me, perhaps I shall have to find some perilous course to cause you both to fret, to make it just."

"I am sure you will think of something." I felt bliss, having finally found my place, and I began to hum a song I had heard in the streets.

"Now come, grab your food and let us begin. I hope you are not too tired to study, having been out all night."

"No, Yhako, I feel as rested as I ever have. In fact, I feel as though I have the energy to study for two or three men!"

"Very well then, perhaps you will, for I am exhausted, and feel inclined to sleep."

"Sleep? Yhako, you have not slept in a decade. You do not even have a bed in this household! Do you remember how it is done?"

"In truth I might not. But it does not matter. I shall not sleep today, for if I have lived this long without it, there be no reason to take it up again now."

"Indeed, brother, perhaps you do need to participate in the revolution, for Ansidrion and I have, and we thrive now as never before."

"No, Federan, I know these actions are not for me. I am an old man now; men like me should step aside as men like you make your way in the world."

"But Yhako, you are the age of Sirlat when she was killed in Grontinion. You have many years left in your life—"

"And I shall use them as I see fit," he retorted. "Federan, you have found what is right for you, and I am glad for it," he continued, softening his tone. "But you and I are different from one another, and we must take different paths. I am content to remain here in my studies, for this is what satisfies me, and it is how I believe I best support this cause."

"Very well. I understand." But I did not believe it. He was defensive because he knew his life was not as purposeful as he had hoped. He had believed in awakening Ilepya, he had believed in bringing about change. But now what did he do toward any of this?

I left for the study, as Yhako was obviously in no mood for such a conversation. He came in a few minutes later with some bread and cheese for me, although he only sipped from a cup of bitter root tea.

"No Ansidrion yet, then?" He asked.

"No, not yet. Perhaps his meeting has gone late. There will be much for them to consider, with the Dictator coming soon."

"Indeed, that seems correct."

We studied in silence for a while, avoiding conversation after the tension we had encountered earlier. I was looking over some old Portavan document, but thoughts of the street protests so distracted me that I could not make much progress. In fact, I had had a difficult time paying much attention to my studies in the last several weeks. It seemed that real change had come to Ilepya—or, at least, the beginning of change. Whether it would blossom into a revolution remained to be seen.

An hour passed. Yhako drank loudly from his tea. "No food for you this morning?" I asked him.

"No, I have not had much of an appetite these days."

I looked at the bread and cheese that lay untouched before me. "I feel little interest in food this morning, either. But you have plenty of appetite for that bitter root tea."

"Yes, well it seems to give me a bit of energy. I have grown used to it now."

We were quiet again. Then a few rays of autumn sunlight peaked through the widow. "It approaches midday now, does it not?" I asked.

"I suppose it does."

I waited for him to say more, but he was silent. So I asked: "Should we have concern for Ansidrion?"

Yhako put his papers down. Yes, perhaps we should."

"Where do they assemble, do you know?"

"I do not, in fact. But it is just as well, for the last thing we would want to do is appear there. If Ansidrion is in any danger, his enemies will be expecting his friends to come calling."

"Well then what shall we do?"

"I am afraid there is nothing." He sighed. "We have nothing but to wait."

"Wait until what? What if he never returns?"

"He will, Federan." He was trying to speak positively, but I knew he was just as concerned as I was.

"Can you consult with your friend who first mentioned the Brotherhood to you? How might we receive any news?"

"Perhaps if we do not hear word by tomorrow morning, I shall go and speak with Beinsar. But he will be fine. Do not worry."

Of course, there was to be no productive time that afternoon. Every sound seemed to me to be a sign of Ansidrion returning. I do not know if Yhako struggled as I did, but he certainly could not have felt serene.

Finally, as dusk arrived, there came a knock at the door. I glanced at Yhako, and I could see he read it as I had. A knock meant unfortunate news; Ansidrion would, of course, have entered without knocking.

Yhako stood and left the study. I sat still for a moment, hoping that if I did not hear what word came by the door, it might not be true. But finally, dreadful curiosity overcame me, and I joined Yhako at the house entry.

"It is impossible to say for sure who has been captured," a short, dour-looking man was explaining. I could not see Yhako's face at all, but the man was clearly distressed, even if trying to sound reassuring. But, of course, the word "captured" was not promising.

"He was present last night. He will have been there, and will have been captured," Yhako said quietly. "Thank you, sir."

"Should any further word come, we shall of course report it to you."

"Thank you," Yhako repeated blankly, and shut the door. He turned to find me watching him intently. He closed his eyes and his voice fell to a whisper. "The *asdesaj* have raided the meeting. We have yet no word how, or the extent, as news has only come from neighbors who witnessed the fracas. A large group of police entered the house, and left a while later, dozens of bound men in tow."

"And what will be done with them?" I asked, desperate. I was seeking reassurance, any sort of suggestion that Ansidrion could survive this. Deep down, I knew what was most likely.

"We might never know for certain. But there is no reason to believe they will not be executed."

I nodded, knowing that there was no arguing. I thought of Ansidrion, imprisoned in doubtlessly horrible conditions, awaiting death. And then I thought of something else, something almost just as awful. "But they will not kill him immediately," I said. Yhako glanced at me, slightly confused but naturally preoccupied. "They have captured a few dozen conspirators. They have valuable information. They will trace Ansidrion to us."

"Ansidrion would not give us up even were they to torture him," Yhako argued, shaking his head.

"But they must have his name in some way. There must be rolls and records in the meeting place. If they see Ansidrion Ponyhubiresh, they will surely know how to find us."

Yhako shrugged. "I suppose we shall see. Time will tell us."

This answer was terrifying and unsatisfactory, but I did not want to say anything more. I was not completely surprised by this, but it was devastating nonetheless. Another sibling gone. Yhako returned to the study, but I remained standing in the entry, tears trickling down my face. I thought of this great house without Ansidrion's boisterous laugh. I thought of the unoccupied desk in the study. I thought of his bedchamber and how it might never be used again. I thought of how much less we might spend on our groceries each week.

Suddenly I became determined that we needed to stop this. He was probably still alive. Perhaps we could join with the street protesters, and the relatives of the other Brotherhood members. I hastened to the study, hoping to rouse Yhako to my side. I found him with his head on his desk. "Yhako!" I said. I thought he had been crying, but I saw, by the way he lifted his head slowly and looked about slightly dazed, that he had been sleeping. "Oh," I whispered. "I…I shall be in my chamber for the night. Please do come to me if you receive any further word."

He nodded but said nothing.

I wanted to think about this monumental change—Yhako and his first bit of sleep in years. But what of freeing Ansidrion? No, it was of no use. We did not even know where he was being kept, and by the time we found him, the *asdesaj* would surely have heard that such a counterattack was coming, and they would have all of the prisoners killed. No, there was nothing to be done. And so I tucked myself into my bed and attempted to sleep. As this was not forthcoming, I repeated the words *yhahram alu* and allowed them to drown out my other thoughts.

The following day, we had a new visitor. He introduced himself as Abhard, and we sat with him in the parlor.

"I am a member of the Brotherhood, and have known Ansidrion, although not closely. First allow me to say that the people of Ilepya owe a great debt to your brother for giving his life that they may have liberty. He is a great martyr."

Yhako and I nodded woefully, but said nothing. Another Ponyhubiresh martyr.

"I am here to narrate to you how this has come to be," Abhard continued. "Perhaps you do not care to hear these details; perhaps they are painful or unimportant to you, and if they are, please interrupt me and I shall leave you in peace."

Again, Yhako and I said nothing.

Abhard continued: "As you may know, the Brotherhood had been planning for our upcoming action, and our meeting had gone rather late. We were preparing to dismiss when there came a great commotion. The door had been brought down, and of a sudden, two dozen armed men—*asdesaj* wielding swords and clubs—swarmed inside. Before we had time to do anything, they hacked five of us to death, perhaps to show their intentions. We were out-manned and out-armed, and there was no use in resisting. A number of us rushed to conceal ourselves, while others attempted to break through the windows to escape.

"The house was surrounded as well, and those who tumbled outside were caught. As far as I know, only two of us survived: I, along with my brother Alimarr, went unnoticed in two large barrels in the basement, waiting for several hours until after the *asdesaj* left.

"They tore the house apart. They took books and papers, stole food and provisions, and simply destroyed what they found of no use. They seemed to have been searching for lists of names or notes. They certainly must have found some of our plans, but you need not worry of names. In meetings we used false identities, and the single list of our true names was kept at a safe house, a mile away. I have that list now, and use it to contact relatives. After this is complete, the list will be destroyed, and there will be no record of your connection to this."

Once again, Yhako and I said nothing for a moment. Then, finally, Yhako shook Abhard's hand, thanked him, and walked away. I escorted the man to the door and shook his hand as well, and then he walked down our little alley, toward Trafgha Street.

But I suddenly felt desperate, despondent about the future. "What is there next?" I called to him.

Abhard turned around to face me once again. "Next?"

"Yes. How does the Brotherhood continue now?"

"It does not. There is no Brotherhood now, young man. It is over." And with that, he walked away, onto the next house of sorrow.

But I knew we needed to start anew. This was a time of despair, of suffering, of peril. But the dire circumstances of life in Ilepya would not change without us taking action. More oppression, more massacres were all we could expect until we made it cease.

For now, however, I did not know how to change a thing. I felt that the need for action was urgent, yet at that same moment, I felt that action was impossible because of my present sadness. I knew that I needed to do something, but I was also powerless. So I returned to the study once again, taking my seat at Yhako's side.

We both sat still in silence for several minutes. After a while, Yhako spoke. "I must go to Grontinion." He turned to me. "I must leave very soon."

"Grontinion? Why must you go to Grontinion? There is nothing for us there." I attempted to sound dismissive of the idea, but in truth it upset me, and I was struggling to repress fear and anger at this sudden declaration.

"No, but there is something for Grontinion here. We need their help, and they will need persuasion to join us. I shall meet with the Chancellor of the University and convince him to send help to us."

"No, let that for someone else. Let others go to Grontinion and speak on our behalf." How could the departure of such a wise man from the center of action be best for our cause?

"But many influential people in Grontinion know my name, and if I go there I shall have their ear. Few other Ilepyans can claim such an advantage."

"Then you will write them letters. There is no need to go there."

"Federan, letters are no longer reliable for matters of this urgency. Word across the borders is not safe, as the government is on watch for treason. Besides, such a conversation consumes time—probably much more time than we have. In the weeks it would require to send a single letter, I can be present, speaking with Chancellor Stahrik in person, already making our case."

"But Yhako, I…" I stopped. I knew I was prepared to tell him I needed him here. But I did not want to say it! I did not want to need Yhako. Ansidrion was gone and I wanted Yhako as close as possible. But Ansidrion was gone and I could lose Yhako just as easily. It was time I learned to be on my own. "I hope you will be safe."

He smiled weakly at me. "I shall, as well as I can. Would you like to accompany me?"

I had not thought of that. Grontinion appealed to me, but not now, not under these conditions. "I do not wish to be apart from you, but I am not ready to leave Ilepya." I thought about the chaos in the streets. These were exciting times in which to be here. They were also dangerous times in which to travel. I wanted to stay, and I feared leaving.

I sighed, and Yhako sensed I was in need of comfort. He placed his arm upon my shoulder. "Then you will be the only Ponyhubiresh who remains in Ilepya for a time. You must and will be a leader here."

I felt a sense of responsibility and perhaps even accomplishment. It was an honor to carry my family name, especially as now it was the family of two respected martyrs. It was remarkable to have lost two of my siblings that way. I began to think of Qhema, once again, and realized that although I had just drafted a letter to her, we had not heard from her in many months. "How do you believe fares Qhema?" I asked Yhako, knowing that he would have no better knowledge than I. But I wanted to speak her name aloud, to make her real again, as all of my attempts at recalling her melody had failed. I wanted to remind myself that we were not alone.

"It is impossible to say. I believe the last letter from her reached this house over eight months ago. Perhaps she will hear of Ansidrion soon. I hope that, when she does, it will be from a friend, for though she sounded full of cheer, I am loath to think of her so alone."

"Indeed, there seems to be very little rest for her these days. I hope that the Vendis with whom she spends her time have the grace to look after her."

"Federan, I am sure it is so." Yhako smiled again, and then stood to begin preparing for his voyage.

The ship that Yhako would board in three days was a trading vessel bound for the city of Hilia, returning from a delivery of foodstuffs. Yhako's passage had been arranged by our friendly grocer, so that he would arouse little suspicion. From Hilia, he would board another ship for Yafia, making landfall at Rakka, and then taking the road inland to Grontinion.

The *asdesaj* still did not keep a particularly close watch on travel, but with the strikes, protests, and now the raid on the Brotherhood, movement became daily more dangerous. Yhako decided it was best to adopt a new identity. "I shall take our father's name—Malqhom, a good, traditional name with ties to all parts of the Great

North. And my surname will be Ehbrud, a Coellic name that will explain my initial travel to Colof. When letters come in this name, know that they are from me."

"And what shall you call me? I hope you will not be writing my name on documents that might fall into the hands of our enemies."

"No, of course not. I shall call you *dofit*, as I always have."

"That is wise," I said. He might just as well call me *dofal*, or brother. After all, there was no other person alive to whom that could refer. I forced a smile, attempting to convince myself we had thought of everything. In reality, we had no idea of what was to come. And it was impossible to fully prepare for anything we were to encounter.

When Yhako left, I did my best to establish normalcy. I took up the household errands, paying for deliveries and signing papers brought by a new *as'shelik* steward. Yhako had arranged affairs such that I never had to leave the house, and the neatness of it all settled me. I declined to visit the tailor or cobbler when a garment needed repair, as I did not like the disruption to routine. I continued studying in the morning, but it held no charm for me. Instead, I looked to the afternoons, when I wrote narrative accounts of my thoughts and actions. These came in the form of letters to Yhako and Qhema, although I knew it would be a long time before I could send them anywhere. I did not even know either of my siblings' locations, but I convinced myself that if I wrote them accounts, they would have to return home someday to read them.

Nevertheless, the most exciting parts of each day came precisely when the day drew to an end. I now spent all of my time in my small bedroom, where I had the best view of Trafgha Street. It was there that, every evening around the hour that the sun disappeared beyond the hills in the distant west, I would begin to hear shouts through my window, and I would smile contently at them. Every night they seemed to grow louder earlier. Although this might merely have been because the cover of darkness crept in at ever earlier hours, I believed it was because the brave protesters of Ilepya were becoming bolder.

I never went into the streets. I had done it once, and had seen the consequences. These protests were not safe for me; two of my siblings were martyrs of the reform, and a third was now essentially an exile, a refugee. If I were recognized on the streets, I would surely be caught and put to death immediately. No, I did my best to remain in the home. Besides, I had important studying and writing to do. My studies helped give intellectual power to the reform, and my writing chronicled these turbulent days for all those who did not live them.

I convinced myself of all of this fairly quickly, and so I found it satisfying to scarcely leave my desk. I received word of the protest as it traveled through the air and into my window at night, as well as through our grocer, whom I learned to trust after he had collaborated with us on Yhako's travels.

As the days passed, snowfall overtook the streets, but this did not slow the protesters' resolve. By late autumn, the protests became so popular that Trafgha Street was no longer merely a conduit to Pariatt and Turka Streets, but rather the site of revolt itself. If I leaned my head out of the window, I could see figures passing by for hours on end, and hear voices chanting for the fall of the government. On the clearest, brightest of nights, I could even identify a few of my neighbors.

This was initially a welcomed development, and I wrote happily to Yhako that it seemed every person in Ilepya must be on the streets. Neither Yhako nor Ansidrion had been particularly supportive of protesting as a political tool, but even to the most skeptical, this news would have been inspiring. I spent hours watching, suffered many a sore neck, craning it so that I could see more. But it was a worthy sacrifice to get a view of what was happening.

But one night, a few weeks short of the year's end, this situation took a grim turn. I had been writing a letter to Qhema when I heard the voices begin that night. I opened the window as usual, and smiled as the protesters by. After a few minutes of this, I noticed Yhonam, the first woman I had met in the streets. Why had neither she nor her cousin Danor not come to ask for more money? I had assumed they had been killed! I wanted to see her again, and I began toward the door.

However, no sooner had I stepped foot out of my bedchamber than I began to hear more shouting. Loud voices were typical by now, but these were sounds of fear and terror, not the predictable anger that had come night after night. And then I heard a word I dreaded: *asdesaj*. The police had come!

I thrust my head back out of the window to survey the streets, but all I saw was chaos. People were running in all directions, and they continued to shout "*asdesaj*" as they ran. Then, a man wearing that familiar blue coat struck another man with a club. Over all of the commotion on the street, I heard the second man cry out in agony before being beaten again. The *desaj* moved on and disappeared into the crowd, likely to beat another protester. But his first victim remained on the ground, wailing at his wounds.

I shuddered as I thought of Ansidrion, who had met his end at the hands of the *asdesaj*. And then I remembered Pelatt, the Noble Laborer from what seemed to be a different lifetime entirely, and how he had suffered a similar fate by the priest. Would the *asdesaj* snuff the light out of these good dissenters, as had happened to Ansidrion and Pelatt?

I heard a pounding at the front door, but I remained at my desk, now frozen in terror. That would be the *asdesaj*, come to drag me out of my home! I thought about the best place to hide, as there came more pounding. Terrible, muddled shouts followed from the street as I crouched beneath my writing table. Minutes passed, although mercifully, no more knocking came at the door. Finally, the yelling began to grow faint, and then ceased altogether. I stood slowly and peered outside of the window once again. Silence and darkness prevailed; I could see no sign of either protesters or *asdesaj*. Had the end come to yet another reform movement? Indeed, it seemed just as Ansidrion predicted it. I decided to resume my letter to Qhema, making note of the tragedy that had just played out before my window, but when I grabbed my pen, I found I could not make the words. No, they were too terrible, and I was too shaken by what had happened. The protests had brought me so much joy, and now any progress we had made against the government would have to begin anew. And to think—I had once considered taking part in them! To what fate might I have succumbed?

Instead, I retreated to my bed and lay awake thinking of the terrible visions I had seen. When the light finally appeared the following day, I hastened to my window again and peered out onto Trafgha Street. It was difficult to see completely from the angle, but there appeared to be a few spots of blood on the stone of the street. Otherwise, however, the road was at peace. I thought of going to call upon my neighbors to ask what they knew, but I worried about what I might hear. No, it was better to live in uncertainty than to confirm the worst.

I trudged through my daily duties that morning, feeling despondent. The afternoon passed by and I made as though to study, although nothing truly entered my brain. As the evening approached and the natural light began to dim, I closed my eyes and sighed heavily, resigned to a sadly silent night. But then, in the distance, I heard a "*yhahram alu.*" Had I imagined it? Was it merely an echo of what I had heard for so many nights? No, I must have created the words in my hope for their recreation. But then I heard it again, and then I saw a man pass by the alley. Was he a fool? Had he come alone? But another followed, and then the "*yhahram alu*" came from a different direction entirely. They had all returned! I grinned. But my smile faded as I recalled the fate they had faced the night before. The *asdesaj* were sure to return. Did they not fear that the attacks would repeat?

I watched with rapt attention. I feared every shout I heard was an alert of the *asdesaj.* For many hours there was no sign of the police, but then finally, around the middle of the night, people began shouting the word, and a high, panicked horn wailed. My body tightened, and I closed my eyes hard. I heard the sound of people running, and a few shouts, and then silence. What had happened? Had the crowds cleared so quickly?

Slowly, I opened my eyes and looked back out of the window. The streets were once again empty, with no sign that any march had occurred. I searched for any evidence of protest or *asdesaj*, but my view was obstructed by the lack of light. After several minutes, I heard a muted, flat horn sound, and then abruptly, people began to appear on the streets once again. The protest continued as though no raid had occurred, and the people even chanted "*yhahram alu*" as they had earlier. The street seemed just as crowded as before. Had they retreated into a safe house? Why had the *asdesaj* been unable to catch them?

Night after night, it continued in this new way. People would protest, a horn would sound, heralding the appearance of the *asdesaj*, and the people would retreat. Then a quieter horn could be heard, and the protesters would return. Some nights there were multiple raids, although on perhaps half of the nights, there was no sign of the *asdesaj* at all, at least on my part of Trafgha Street. I felt a bit ashamed that, although I considered myself a leading member of the opposition by virtue of my brothers, I still did not understand how this process worked. I asked the grocer, but he did not know, and again, I did not dare venture outside of my home to learn. Yet careful observation yielded me nothing.

I spent every hour of every night with my head out of the window, watching carefully, hoping for some sign of progress. During the day, I struggled to remain awake—apparently I could not thrive without sleep, as Yhako had for so many years. So I caught some rest for a half hour here or an hour there. One afternoon, I awoke from a brief nap to a polite knock at the door. It could not be the grocer; he had come just two days before, and I did not entertain any other guests in those days. I worried that it was the *asdesaj*, and so I sat up, prostrate, frozen in fear, attempting to make as little noise as possible.

The knock came a second time, but I did not yield to it. Several minutes more passed before I decided that whoever it was had retreated, and that I was safe to move about the house. I continued in my daily duties, and watched the protests as usual that night. The following afternoon, the *as'shelik* steward came, and I signed several orders. "And there is this, as well," he said, handing me a folded document, closed with a ribbon and wax. "I found it in the alley before your door."

I took the note and examined it, but the outside betrayed nothing of its contents. "What is this?" I wondered aloud. I broke the seal and read the first line. *To the Honored* Dofit.... Could it be? Yhako! "Is there anything else for me to sign?" I asked, hastily.

"No sir, that is all. Good day to you."

He left and I eagerly opened the letter again.

To the Honored Dofit:

With joy I inform you of my arrival in the city of Rakka. I intend to begin on the road to Grontinion henceforth, as there are already Ilepyans laboring here in Rakka on our behalf. However, I have passed a day here, touring the city with a local alderman who is supportive of our purpose.

When I left you, dofit, *you appeared to be in as good of spirits as you could be, with a full understanding of our cause. If you have since wavered, I shall tell you what I have witnessed in Rakka, as it has renewed my belief wholly. Since my arrival I have not seen a single person discontent, nor anyone having to survive with less than he or she need. The streets are free of crime and the public squares are full of people making merry. This afternoon my host, Karliott, has brought me to Etta Va Square, the largest plaza in the city. During the height of the revolution, many battles took place here, and it was not unusual in those days to stumble across a body in these streets. Today, I found people taking meals in public with friends, discussing reformist theology over a game of cards. I have witnessed hope, as honest people seek to make a place of destruction into a place of rebirth. It has inspired me.*

Dofit, *I must confess to you that I had begun to suffer a loss of clarity and belief in our purpose. We had lost our brother and sister, but what had we gained? They had sacrificed so much for the good of others, and had seen nothing good come of it. Our beloved brother had done just fine practicing his faith in private for so many years! Why did he need to take such risks? He could have been content for all of his life. Instead, he joined that secret affinity to allow for others the same freedoms he had, and in this he met no success and lost everything.*

What was the reason? Nothing had changed because of his actions, but that he lost his life. I fled Ilepya because I could no longer tolerate being in that place of sorrow, that place of no progress. I came to Rakka in search of revenge; my brother had been killed so I wanted to recruit others to inflict pain upon his killers. Hatred and indifference had filled my heart, and I became disconnected from my cause and careless about the result. I no longer felt interested in change. Karliott has informed me that this was common during the revolution here: becoming so exhausted from the pains of the fight as to wish to give up.

But dofit, Karliott has become my prophet, and his prophecy is this: do not allow the difficulty of the task before you to frighten you from completing it. You must fight this cowardice within you, and in doing so, inspire those around you out of their complacency. This simple message has refreshed my belief in the cause of revolution. I have seen it manifested in Rakka, which shows what we can achieve if we shall only keep fighting for it. If you are in need of renewal, allow Karliott to be your prophet, and this message to be your prophecy.

My resolution doubled, I shall continue on the road to Grontinion tomorrow, writing to you as often as I can. Let you continue to be strong, as I know you are, brother. I love you, and shall see you soon in success.

From Rakka, this 1ˢᵗ day of Astavfashesh
Your Humble Brother, Malqhom Ehbrud

I let the letter drop from my hands and onto the desk. These were exactly the words I had needed to hear, and for this reason, I had not wanted to hear them. The letter caused my ignorance to dissipate, and the terrible shackles of my misguided focus to fall to the ground. I finally realized now what I should have known for two months—my actions had been useless. To avoid the fate that Ansidrion had met, I had retreated into a prolonged state of fearful inaction. I had not lost interest in the cause, like Yhako had; I had instead been cowed from doing anything about it.

What good were the ideas that I spent all day studying and writing, without action? This was the very thing I had criticized Yhako for, yet now here I was, waiting for my neighbors to bring my ideas into practice. I had convinced myself that this was acceptable. I had, out of fear, allowed myself to believe that a decaying city in which residents kill each other in the streets was something I could not be bothered to rectify. Spending each day and night in my bedroom had been satisfactory enough for me to rebuff what was great. But the great was achievable!

It was an illuminating prophecy. I could do more. We could all be free. The discovery was so inspiring that it was terrifying to hold. So much was possible that I felt as though to not do everything would be to fail. My potential, the potential of my fellow Ilepyans, intimidated me.

I decided to begin immediately. If I were so daunted by what could be done, why should I not set to work right at this moment? But thinking on what I needed to do drew the blood from my head and all of my limbs into my heart, and I felt weak and immobile. Undertaking even one of the tasks facing me meant exposing myself to the violence which I so opposed. The streets were a place of danger, a place of brutality, a place in which people were attacked merely for their beliefs. I knew that what I stood to gain was great, but it was difficult to shrug off my fear.

Voices sounded from the streets now, as the sun had retreated to its home for the evening. Even from my chamber, with my windows shuttered, I could hear cries of "*peilav kelgarim*—the people demand liberty."

"Throw aside your cowardice," I commanded myself, "for it is a tool of the oppressors, placed in your heart, in order that you might not take action against them." The time had come to join my fellow protesters once again, and so, despite the persisting weight of fear throughout my body, I threw myself onto my feet and burst out of the front door.

I ran down the alley and joined the dozen men and women on Trafgha Street. I was renewed, and felt as though I had already won the first battle of the night by fighting the complacency within me. "*Yhahram alu,*" I shouted. The light is with me. The people around me repeated these words. For a minute the street rang with the sound, and it spread across Ilepya. I smiled as I thought of others, trapped by fear inside of their homes. Hearing this phrase would surely give some person comfort, and in this case, it originated with me. I was but one of a thousand on the streets that night, but each of us could call ourselves a hero of the revolution.

I walked amongst the others with a steady stride toward where Pariatt and Turka Streets met. The number of protesters had multiplied since I had last left the house, and I found myself fighting my way through crowds. Then, almost as soon as I reached Malqhom Street, I spotted an unmistakable face amongst the protesters. The face belonged to a man of shorter stature, with tattered clothing and a slow, measured limp. He was conspicuous, but perhaps merely because I knew how special he was; how he was a man whom I would never forget. Aside from my brothers, who were either deceased or many miles away, he was the man I most longed to see.

I pushed my way through the others and approached him. I grasped his arm tightly, but this startled him and he jumped, and then he grimaced because of the pain in his leg. "Pelatt? Hello, Pelatt, do you remember me?"

The Noble Laborer looked at my shoes and trousers, and then upon my shirt, and then cast his gaze upon the hand that clutched his arm. As soon as he looked into my eyes, his face transformed itself with what appeared to be delighted surprise. "The young boy! The priest's boy, the boy who rescued me!"

"Rescued I would not say," I responded, smiling. "But yes, I am that old priest's boy. I am glad to see you have lived, and that you appear to be as happy and good as always." I had so longed to see him that I did not know quite what to say, and I felt overwhelmed by the joy and poignancy of the moment. The Noble Laborer stood before me. He had been corrupted by Ma't's words, and broken by his actions, but now I had access to him once again. "What do you here, at the protests?"

"I have come here because those who have given me sustenance and love are here. Every day I join these young men and women in the streets because they smile at me and shake my hand, and sometimes allow me to rest in their homes. Those who employ me in small tasks in exchange for room or a few *diyar* coins are only those who protest here, and so I assume this must be a meeting of charitable souls, whom I aspire to join." He still spoke slowly, and seemed as simple as ever. He had seen more of the world since I had first met him, of course, but it did not seem to affect him in any way other than his physical well-being, which was obviously still harmed by the attack.

"And how do you occupy your days? What do you do for labor?"

"I can work as I had no longer, with this leg. I take on a few minor tasks for my bread, such as cleaning a home or looking after stock, but my condition is such that I cannot do any one thing for a term, and instead must search for an odd task here and there."

"I am most sorry, Pelatt, for you have suffered that grievous wound through no fault of your own, and I must take responsibility for how it was dispensed unto you."

"There be no reason to apologize, young...now *I* must apologize, for I do not even know your name!"

"Ah, no such regrets necessary. My name is Federan, although I most often shorten it to Fe'n."

"I am glad to finally know it, for I have always wondered the title of that virtuous young person who saved my life. You were but a boy then, but are a man now." He smiled at me and I shrugged in response. "Oh, and here I am without manners once again." He grabbed my right hand and shook it. "My name is Pelatt, as you know. And it is my pleasure to meet you, Fe'n, forever in whose debt I am."

"No debt, sir Pelatt, no debt at all. But tell me, when you do not find an employer to take you in, and when you do not spend your nights here, where do you rest?"

"I do very little of that." He pressed his lips together and looked at me frankly. "When I need rest but have no indoor place for it, I merely find a nice spot of grass or hay near the coast and catch a few minutes of peace."

"You must stay with me!" I insisted. "It is not right for you to live on the streets, as you are a great man and a man to whom I am indebted."

But Pelatt shook his head. "No, sir, I cannot. I do not call in debts to innocent young men, especially as I have done nothing for your gratitude. I have survived on the streets for this long, and so I shall continue. But I thank you for your kindness."

"No! You must; I shall not allow you to decline. I have plenty of space in my home, and you deserve a warm place to rest your head."

But he seemed unconvinced. "There are many in these streets who have greater need than I. Go and choose one of them."

His nobility had driven him to the point of stubbornness. "If you will not do it for your own well-being, then please do it for mine. My brothers have died or fled, and I live alone now. I need a merry man like you to cheer my company."

Pelatt frowned and then pursed his lips. Finally, he smiled. "Very well then, as you have saved my life, I owe you this favor. But at the moment that you have grown tired of my company or can no longer keep me, you must announce it, and I shall leave at once."

"That I promise." I smiled back at him. And then I grabbed the man's right arm and threw it over my shoulder, allowing him to shift his weight off of his bad leg and onto me as we walked toward Trafgha Street.

We arrived perhaps half an hour later, as noble Pelatt had had to walk slowly and take many breaks. I supported him as well as I could, but even though he was a fairly small man, he was still much more weight than I was accustomed to carrying. When we finally entered the door of my home, I led him to the most comfortable seat, and boiled some water to make sweet root tea. He took a sip of it and formed that familiar frown, his dark, heavy brows casting themselves over his eyes. Then, as he would often do, he smiled.

"Do you enjoy the tea?" I asked. "I am sorry if it is not what you prefer to drink, but it is either that or the bitter root."

"Do not be sorry; it is just fine. It is warm, and that is enough for me."

"How do you feel? You must be hungry. What might I prepare for you?"

"Oh, you do not need to give me food. Shelter is enough charity from you."

"No, Pelatt, do not be humble!" I laughed, frustrated with his unrelenting goodness. "I have plenty, and can give you whatever you desire. My brother Yhako has saved a great fortune in his life, and there be nothing better to spend it on than your wellness."

"Very well, but I do not care much to eat."

"Come, Pelatt, I shall hear no more argument on the matter, for it is good to have a bit of sustenance after a long day." I went to the cupboard and grabbed a pair of apples and some bread, but when I held them in my hands, I found that they had no appeal to me. "I suppose I understand how you feel now," I told him. "I have not eaten in many hours, yet my stomach carries on as though contented."

He merely smiled in response.

"But beyond that, I shall make a bed available to you," I continued. "My brother Ansidrion still has a bed in this home, and it has not been occupied for many nights." I swallowed against a welling of sorrow in my throat. "You will make use of this bed, for it serves no other purpose."

"No, Fe'n, I shall not. The floor of your home will suffice for me."

"Oh come, Pelatt!" I scolded him but could not suppress my smile. "Please allow me to show you kindness. Accept my generosity. There are two beds in this home and two of us staying here now, so there be no reason either of us should sleep on the floor."

"Those are the beds of great men. I have not earned the honor to even stay in this home, and it is unthinkable that I should sleep where they have slept. No, in this household the beds will be used only by those who have earned them, and humble I have not done anything of their worth."

"You have suffered through many of your years, Pelatt. You have lived on the streets, have been severely injured. Merely by being a human, a person of good honor, you have earned the right to occupy one of those chambers."

"Fe'n, you are correct to say that I have lived on the streets. I have done so all my life! I have never taken sleep in a bed and have done just fine thus far. I have no need for it, but will instead sleep as your loyal servant should: on the floor at your feet."

I thought this outrageous, but Pelatt insisted upon it. "Very well, if you will accept nothing else, I suppose there can be no discussion about it. But you must allow me to place a cushion there, that you might have a bit of comfort."

"If these are the terms under which we might compromise, so let it be. I shall take your cushion. Thank you, gracious Fe'n."

"No, thank you, gentle Pelatt." As it was now late at night, and therefore it was shortly becoming time for us to sleep, I found a few pillows and assembled them at the foot of my bed. Pelatt came and laid himself down upon them. He appeared to fall asleep instantly, closing his peaceful eyes and slowing his breath. But no sooner had I gotten into bed and shut my eyes than Pelatt began to speak.

"Fe'n, what think you of the *tarbhasht?*" He asked me.

"What is there to think of it? I support labor strikes, whether it is the port workers or the timberers, or anyone else in this city. I only wish I were working in some sort of labor, so that I, myself, might strike."

"But do you believe the *tarbhasht* succeeds? Do you think it is enough?"

I thought for a moment. "It does succeed. But it is not enough. The Ilepyan civil society is too weak. Yes, by ceasing to labor in the state's ports, mines, and timber yards, we reduce their profits, but we have yet to sufficiently embarrass the government, to fully tarnish its legitimacy. Why have you asked of it? Do you have concerns?"

"No, no concerns. These are the sorts of things I think of. I do not know much about the *tarbhasht* or about the protests, but I spend many hours wondering about them. I apologize if I trouble you now with these questions."

"Not at all, Pelatt." I was finding that my body had little desire for sleep, as I felt in no manner tired. "I am glad to share with you any knowledge I have, as long as you are willing to do the same."

"Of course, sir, although I confess I have very little. But if the *tarbhasht* is unable to affect those who lead the government, what might do better?"

I sighed. "I do not know." If I had known, we would have done it already, and perhaps have achieved much more by now.

"Apologies, Fe'n, for I know you have gone many hours without sleep, and perhaps desire a rest free of the *tarbhasht.*"

"It is fine, Pelatt. I understand."

We were silent once again, as he allowed me to seek sleep. But now I was certain that this was the thing my body required least. "It sounds as though the protests continue at this hour," I remarked.

"Indeed, they usually remain until close to dawn."

He was likely thinking the same thing I was, so I spoke it: "Then why have we come here? If others still protest now, should we not?"

"I had thought the same thing, but did not want to rouse you if you were tired."

"No, I desire sleep less than I ever have." I stood from my bed abruptly and dressed myself once again. Pelatt did likewise. "Back to Turka Street, then," I said smiling.

So we returned to the streets, standing with our neighbors, calling for change. When we came home early the next morning, just before dawn, Pelatt finally explained the horns to me. "I have learned it from the others on the streets. The high horn means the *asdesaj* are coming, while the flat horn means that they have left."

Yes, I had assumed this much. "But who carries the horn?"

"Word has it that one protester has a horn-maker cousin who has donated them to the cause. Sympathetic families who own homes near major street corners hold them, and they watch from their windows and alert of the *asdesaj*."

"I suppose it is good to have friends in many different industries." Would that I knew more about the *as'shelik*, and could provide them for some purpose. "Then when the horn is blown, where do the protesters find shelter?"

"It has been difficult. Many do not find any respite whatsoever. But there are sufficient protesters that usually at least one lives nearby and can let us into his or her home, if a horn is blown while the *asdesaj* remain out of view. But most often, we merely run from emptier streets to the larger, central streets, where we outnumber the *asdesaj* most. If a group of twelve of them appears with clubs, they might easily take on twenty or thirty of us. But imagine the several hundred people it needs to fill up Turka Street. The *asdesaj* does not dare attack us when we number so many."

"So there is some coordination now. The people are not merely acting alongside one another, but working together." Pelatt nodded. Ansidrion would be proud. Yhako would be in awe.

Within days of Pelatt taking up residence in the home, strange things began to occur. When I first discovered him, I could see that his shirt and pants were little more than rags, having been soiled with the sweat and dirt that came from consecutive use on the streets. So I made him put on some of my clothes as I had his things washed and mended. I was several inches taller than he, and probably had twenty pounds on him besides, so the clothes fit a bit loosely when he first put them on. But several days later, after he had returned them to me, I was surprised to find that they no longer suited me.

"How have you done this?" I asked him, smiling. "What trick or craft is this?"

But he seemed puzzled at my questions, and claimed to have done nothing.

"Look, Pelatt! This shirt now hugs so closely upon my chest! The pant legs hover two inches above the ground. What have you done to shrink them so?"

He frowned. "Those clothes were too large for me. How can they be so small on you?"

I stared at him in bewilderment. "Here, let you have them, for they are no longer of any use to me."

So Pelatt left my presence to don these mysterious articles. He returned after several minutes with a smile upon his face. "Good Fe'n, they fit perfectly. How can this be?"

Just as he said, the clothes fit his body as though they had been sewn for him, contrary to what had been true but days before. "Have you altered them?" I asked. "Have we both grown?"

But Pelatt was at just as much of a loss as I. "It is but one of many, many wonders we encounter in a day," he said, shrugging. I thought he must have arranged for this in some manner, but I could not figure out how, and he refused to betray any proof of it.

The following day, the mechanical clock that Yhako had imported from Acrola ceased its function. I went to wind it just as he had taught me, but this did nothing aside from producing a strange, frustrated ticking sound. I did not know of a single clocksmith in the country, let alone one that used parts that complied with the boycott rules of the *evatarr*, so I opened the thing up and poked around. I had seen inside of it a few times before under Yhako's supervision, so I knew at once that what I saw before me was wrong. The iron cogs that exercised their influence over the timepiece had all fallen out of place, and a few even rolled toward me, out of the clock, as I opened the pane. There was nothing I could do to fix them, so I merely scooped up all of the loose gears and placed them back within the clock.

I would not have thought much of the clock, but that it happened so soon after the shrinking clothes. I immediately suspected Pelatt, only because I knew that such things required human agency, and he was the only other person who had been in the house. Did he sabotage me? Did his gentle, gracious demeanor conceal something dark? Perhaps he had not forgiven me for what Ma't had done after all, and he had merely infiltrated my home in order to harm me. Of course, one could do many worse things than alter a pair of clothes or break a clock, but I could think of no other explanation for it, so I went directly to Pelatt to ask him.

Once again, he expressed his gentle innocence perfectly. "I have never touched that machine before, as I do not even know what purpose it serves."

"You did not meddle with the cogs within?" I demanded.

"No, good Fe'n." He shook his head. "I do not know what a cog is."

There was absolutely no explanation for this beyond his sabotage, and yet, I found that I believed him. His nature was so calm, his innocence so total, that I had trouble understanding how he could even have conceived of such tricks. "Very well, then," I said. "I suppose it is another of your wonders." I shook my head and he shrugged his shoulders—a little dance that would become a defining gesture of our relationship.

In fact, we would repeat it not four days later. I had taken to teaching Pelatt how to write the alphabet, and he would practice writing words as I undertook my studies. He seemed to enjoy the task, and one afternoon, I even overheard him hum a little melody as he worked. I looked up and smiled. "So you are enjoying yourself, are you? It has been many years since I heard happy music in this house."

He returned the smile, but said nothing, continuing with the gentle song. I resumed reading for a moment, but then I remembered something.

"Where have you learned that song?" I demanded, my eyes flashing at him.

He frowned. "I do not know. I feel as though I have always known it. I must have heard someone sing it long ago, and I have repeated it to myself ever since."

"*Down the path we have begun,*" I sang along to the tune he had made. "It is the song Qhema sang to me!"

"Qhema?"

"My sister. She looked after me when I was young, and sang the most beautiful notes to me. There were a few different tunes, but that was my favorite. I had lost it, forgotten it in recent years, but I know that is the song."

"Perhaps it is a popular song among Ilepyans." He shrugged.

"Yes, perhaps it is." But even so, I regarded this as yet one more sign of his mystique. Of course this, like the clock and the clothes, could only be due to worldly chance. Yet I found myself convinced that Pelatt's arrival must have been associated somehow with all of these wondrous miracles. It was proof that he was the true Noble Laborer, sent to me with knowledge that I was destined to receive. I took his advice as absolute truth, and trusted him in all things.

I was to discover, but a few days later, that he was, in fact, the one who broke the mechanical clock, although not by design. We had ceased to be touched by hunger, and thus no longer ate, but I still insisted on spending some time at the table each day with food before us. "Perhaps one day our bodies should suddenly gather an appetite," I had said, "and, having been so long without, would abruptly need all the food we have in the house." And so, the table fully set, Pelatt and I sat down one evening to speak over bowls of soup.

I cannot remember exactly what we had been speaking of just then. It was likely excited discussion of the protests we would engage in later that night. But whatever I had been saying, I dropped it immediately, as I noticed the fork before Pelatt slowly wriggling about on the table. It was a subtle movement, such that I had to stare for several seconds to ensure that it was not merely a trick of my eye. But no, even upon the closest inspection, I could see that not only was the fork moving, but it was slowly creeping toward my companion.

"Pelatt, behold the fork! It is drawn unto you!"

As usual, the man merely shrugged. "As it will, for as many forks have."

I grabbed the utensil and found it devoid of life as always. But as I moved it toward Pelatt, I felt it pull itself with so slight a force that I might not have noticed it had I not expected it. I placed it against his chest and it rested there for a moment before he shook and it fell loose. Then I grabbed my fork and we repeated these same wonders. "Pelatt, you have the lure! You hold sway over metal as though a magnet."

"So it has been," he said, smiling. "I have never been able to evade it although, mercifully, it has not had a dramatic impact upon me."

Indeed, it could not have been particularly strong, as I had never seen a cluster of irons trailing him about the house. But I determined that it had been strong enough to damage the clock. His presence as he had walked past it many times, perhaps standing before it for several minutes to divine its function, had been enough to draw the cogs out of their place. This power had little practical use that I could discover, but it was yet another sign his mysterious enchantment.

Yet, when I spoke of this to him, he deferred it, and refused to believe that there was anything special about him. "I am but a simple man who has learned very little in life. I possess a rare quality in the lure, but this is merely a purposeless chance of birth, just as you have greater stature and a fuller beard. I have never been in awe of you for those things, and so you should not be in awe of me for this."

"But my size and hair are not coincidences, but due to my family. I am of larger build and hairier chin because so was my father, and so were my brothers Yhako and Ansidrion. Did your father or brothers possess the lure?"

"I have never met another who has it, but what does it matter? Have your brothers healed other people the way that you have healed me?"

"I have done nothing more than take you into my home, which is exactly as they would have done. I am sure that they have adopted many people into their care, and that Yhako will do so many more times."

"No, not merely that." Pelatt beamed. "You are a particular man of miracles, and have wrought wonders far greater than I. In the years since I first received my injuries, I had scarcely recovered at all, and could not have walked without use of a cane. But in these days, not two weeks in your home, my restoration has continued and accelerated greatly." And at this, just as I had begun to frown in confusion, he put himself to his feet. With seeming effortlessness, he walked from his seat to the door, and then back, without use of the walking stick or any other aid.

"Pelatt, this is a miracle! How can you have achieved such a thing?"

"I have done nothing," he insisted with a smile. "But your gracious care and wondrous presence have allowed me to heal fully, and regain my strength. I can walk again, Fe'n. And look here upon my leg." He adjusted his pants such that I could see his thigh where he had been struck. "The wound and its scar are gone. It is exactly as though I never met that priest."

I stood beside him in awe, unable to believe the many miracles that had come to happen all around me. "It is good that you are here, Pelatt. We have each helped the other find his way."

* * * *

After a few days more of protesting, I realized that the horn-maker had had it right. We needed to keep our resources together, to share amongst one another. "Have you heard of the ewitterada, in Yafia?" I asked Pelatt.

But Pelatt could not say the word, for it used sounds that were to his tongue unknown.

"No, of course you will not have," I said. "It is known as evatarr in Galmostan: boycott. Avoiding commerce with those whose policies oppose yours."

"I have not heard of this, but it has sense."

"The Ilepyan Brotherhood used the *evatarr*, and we continue to comply with it as well as we can today. But what if we specifically direct our money to reformists? My grocer supports reform; perhaps every reformist should prefer him. I do not know to where my money goes, but I should."

"Indeed. Might we make a list of those protesters we know who have businesses? And might we prefer them for such transactions?"

"Yes, we should prefer them. Preference," I said, satisfied with myself. "Parebhur."

"Then let us ask our friends among the protesters how they are in need. Let us give them our support."

"Yes, but I believe we can do even more than that."

The following day, I decided to pay a visit to Dena Beinsar, the sister and former partner of the cobbler who had been killed alongside Ansidrion, to buy some shoes for Pelatt. The shoes were important, of course, but as soon as the order had been made, I began in on a new conversation.

"Madam, I have seen you protest alongside us in the street many nights, is it so?"

"Yes, it is true, I do spend my nights there," she agreed.

"So you believe in the need for reform? And do you have friends who do the same?"

Then Dena paused. "What does it mean to you? What do you want with my friends?"

"I wish to give them my business. My grocer, for example, believes in the reform, as do you, my cobbler. But if there be trustworthy tailors, candle-makers, carvers and so on, I should prefer their business over others."

"Hum." Dena was silent for a moment. "My neighbor in the house just east of this is a tailor, and I have seen him return here in the morning alongside me. I do believe he protests, as well."

"Very well, madam, thank you. He will now be my tailor. And if you should mistrust your grocer, let you pay a visit to mine."

"I do not use the services of a grocer, but I shall spread his name amongst my reformer friends, and he will surely gain their business."

I thanked the woman and provided her with the grocer's name and where he lived. Then I went to the tailor's house and performed the same such action, explaining to him who deserved his business and for what cause. And so Pelatt and I continued, going to home and business again and again, spreading our contacts and enacting the *parebhur*. It was more of a commercial agreement among friends, much smaller than the *tarbhasht* or *evatarr* had been. But I was determined to do my part. I felt satisfied knowing that my money was only going to those that supported my causes, that it could not fall into the hands of the *asdesaj*, used to attack innocent protesters.

* * * *

One night, perhaps a week after the little *parebhur* had begun, we heard some protesters near Iromal Street cursing the Iqharepur, calling him evil, greedy, and unlawful. This was, of course, a normal sentiment amongst protesters, but it was rarely the center of protest cries.

"What has he done yet?" I asked a particularly angry man. "Why do we worry ourselves with his name tonight?"

"He is always worthy of disdain, but tonight we have received word of yet another of his horrendous acts." The man was full of rage, and seemed as though he was waiting for someone to ask him this very question, so that he could recount the deed. "Assassins in Pondital have murdered a dozen brave protesters in the streets. Of course, these killers are in the employ of the Iqharepur, who pays them with money he has wrenched from us. But some of them were caught, and found to have been carrying papers with the Iqharepur's seal on them! In every way he can, he sanctions these terrible murders of honest Hihaytheans."

I shook my head. This was no surprise, but killing of our companions was never welcome news. Pondital was a town outside Ilepya, and as our city had turned in favor of reform, that town had followed. But as it was much smaller, the government could more easily overwhelm the protesters there with greater numbers of *asdesaj*, making the residents there subject to more violence than we were.

We continued passing through the crowds, but Pelatt grabbed at my sleeve. "Fe'n," he said, looking at the street beneath our feet. "I must ask you a question that you will think is foolish."

"Nonsense, Pelatt," I told him. "You may ask me whatever you will."

"Nonsense, indeed, young Fe'n, for I am ignorant of something I should well not be. I must confess that I do not know what exactly the Iqharepur is." He shrugged as he looked at me, as was his custom.

"Do not know?" I asked, incredulous. "But have we not taken to these streets, week after week, to speak out against him? How can you not know what you so strongly oppose?"

"Apologies, Fe'n, but I do not believe that is the case. I have never once spoken out against the Iqharepur, as I choose to remain silent on subjects of which I am ignorant. I only hear the passionate cries of those around me, and know that he must be terrible, but do not know why."

This seemed not to make any sense to me at all. We protested every night because of the Iqharepur. "If not for the Iqharepur, then why do you come here?"

"Because every person I have met who takes part in or supports these protests is good. The people I admire—you and your siblings, the people at the *deshilva* school who kept my company before my injury, the people who employed me when I was capable of very little—these are all members of the reform. And when I think of persons who have done terrible things—that old priest of yours, the vandals who break windows at schools, the bandits who attack lingering protesters— these are all members or supporters of the government. I am not philosophical like you, Fe'n. I cannot understand all of the thought and history behind this movement. But I do understand liberty, and charity, and generosity, and I know these to be qualities of those who support the reform."

"But the doctrine? The priests, the church, the religion? These mean nothing to you?"

"They do not. I have never given much thought to these things, except when those around me mention what corruption the church supports. I do not believe that the church needs to remain, nor that it should be overthrown. It can do whatever it likes, as long as it permits liberty for those around it. If the church supports the oppression of Ilepya, I shall oppose the church. But if it gives this up; if it is in favor of liberty, charity, and generosity, then I shall embrace and love it as a part of Hihaythean society."

"Perhaps it is merely that you do not know the evils of this church," I argued, "for surely if you did, you would not hesitate to speak out against it."

"I do not believe this is the case, Fe'n, but we may try it. What are the great crimes of the church that I should oppose?"

"There is the selection of the Iqharepur, of course! Do you know that, most often, when one Iqharepur dies, he is succeeded by his son? Even on occasions when that son is merely a child! How can a young, illiterate boy be capable of divining the Order before the rest of us?"

"That I cannot answer, Fe'n. I do not give much thought to it."

"Or, indeed, what of the Lords' Occult? Know you much of that worship?"

"The Seven Lords, is it not?"

"Yes, the Lords' Occult is the church's sanctioned worship of the Seven Lords. These were men who achieved success in war, and some in politics thereafter. And for this their spirits are to be treated as intercessors? Men to whom we should pray, who can subvert the Order when we find that its will is distasteful?"

Pelatt shrugged. "It could be. Or it could not be."

"But is it? Do you agree or do you disagree?"

"Good Fe'n, I do not know what an intercessor is, but this is not a concern for me, as I do not think much of these things. Do I believe that these dead Seven Lords go about subverting the Order on my behalf, or could do so, if I were willing to pray to them? I should hope not, as I do not even know all of their names, or how to pray!"

"There, then! You do not believe it. You know it is wrong."

"I do not believe it, indeed. But I cannot know. There might be many things about this world of which I am not aware. Who am I to decide for others whether they are true or not?"

"But some things must be true. Some things are so clearly false, and they must not be sustained." People continued to pass us and curse the Iqharepur, but I was so enthralled by Pelatt's disinterest that I had forgotten about the protest entirely.

"Even if I were to believe these things," he went on, "what harm would it do to anyone else?"

"But it is wrong!"

"And if you are so certain, then tell them it is wrong. And if they refuse to hear you, then let them be wrong. There be no point in concerning ourselves so with the beliefs of others."

"Yes, that is good, until I tell a *desaj* how they believe wrong, and I am murdered just as Sirlat was."

"Which is precisely where we have begun, good Fe'n. I believe in your right to reject the Lords' Occult, just as I believe in another person's right to accept it. And so in support of that right, I come to the street. We cannot bring down one government in support of freedom for ourselves, and then usher in a new government that would deny the selfsame freedom to anyone else."

"Liberty, charity, and generosity," I repeated. As always, Pelatt's message was simple enough. But was it too simple for reality? For, just as he had described, those of the old religion opposed the revolt, and the reformers supported it. If we brought about a new government that permitted those who rejected religious reform to practice freely, would they not merely agitate for the old, until our new society built on Pelatt's simple ideals collapsed?

Had this movement never been about religion? What would Yhako think? He had gone to Grontinion to seek support from those who had led the religious reform movement. Or had he gone there merely because we had connections in that city, and because Grontinion had already carried out a political reform?

I thought about the Ilepyan Brotherhood. They certainly would agree with Pelatt's belief in liberty, charity, and generosity at its face. But would they permit such liberty as to allow the old faith to carry on as it had? Certainly, all of the members of the Brotherhood would have been of the reform, and were likely of a mind to enforce it on others. I saw no separation between the reforms of religion and government, and thus it must be necessary to have the former if the latter was to be achieved.

We continued marching through the streets that night, but Pelatt had given me much to think about, and I admit I was deeply distracted. When the dawn came, and Pelatt and I returned home to Trafgha Street, we said nothing to one another. Perhaps I had given him as much to think about as he had given me, or perhaps his mind were as simple as always—thinking merely of liberty, charity, and generosity.

The *asdesaj* began to appear less and less. Where before, in high winter, we had encountered them in groups of six perhaps every other day, now they came in three or four, and we saw them but once a week. The nights—and, thus, the hours of relative safety in the streets—were slowly drawing shorter, yet we felt more emboldened than ever. The cold was less stifling, and our neighbors found fewer excuses to stay in their homes at night.

We allowed the *asdesaj* to give us less chase. I noticed it in particular on the first night of spring, when I heard the high horn somewhere along Pariatt Street. A few of us casually rounded a corner and then poked our heads back around Pariatt to see the enemy's numbers. "I say four today," one man suggested at a normal volume.

I turned to get a look at him. "No, they will be weak this night," his friend responded. "No more than three, although I expect two."

"Perhaps it is not the *asdesaj* at all, but merely a strange man stumbling home from visiting his lover at this hour." These two men, and a few others with us, chuckled.

"It has become so," I whispered to Pelatt. "The *asdesaj* no longer give us fear, but we openly mock them." I realized at that moment that we had become an insurmountable force; we had already turned the tide too strongly against our opponents. "It is only a matter of time before they abandon the city entirely."

"What will come next, then?" Pelatt asked. "Will that be the end of our fight?"

"I suppose it shall. Perhaps the government in Poonlon will send a force to fight us, but I believe by that time we shall have become so entrenched as to be invincible. We must soon begin to go about establishing our own free government."

"And what will that government be?"

The *asdesaj*—and there had been three of them—had, by this time, appeared at the other end of the block, and merely passed by along the nearby corner. Our fellows had begun to wander back out onto Pariatt Street, even without having heard the flat horn.

"I do not know yet, Pelatt. I suppose it might take a form similar to the new government in Yafia, where the people all assemble and choose their leaders without pressure from others. But I know that it must be guided by those principles that you first spoke to me: liberty, charity, and generosity."

Pelatt nodded slowly, and no sooner had the flat horn sounded than I heard voices behind us, to the north. "There are protesters as far north as Kalal Street?" I asked, surprised. I motioned to Pelatt for us to examine further.

Sure enough, this block—although much more thinly-populated than Pariatt Street—was the site of protests as well. We were perhaps three miles from the timber yards, where the protests had begun. "I wonder if there is any place left in Ilepya untouched by our cries." I said to Pelatt.

"If we travel much further northeast, we shall come to the place where the port workers live, and they surely will join us when they hear the words *yhahram alu*." And then a light grew in his eyes, and he took a step in that exact northeasterly direction.

"Pelatt, is it right? Is it safe?"

A grin overcame his face, and then he turned entirely and began to walk along Kalal Street, in the direction of the former school, in a way that would eventually lead to the port. I gasped, but followed him eagerly, allowing the excitement to take control of me.

We passed Malqhom Street, and seemed to be the only protesters in the area. The streets were dark, and my heart raced faster than my feet. Could we awaken all of the port workers? Perhaps with their strength, tonight, we could take the Bishop's palace at the Apgha!

But then I heard a host of footsteps, and words in a foreign tongue. I saw a row of familiar blue coats before us. There were a dozen *asdesaj!* "Pelatt!" I screamed. I grabbed his arm and pulled him west again, back toward the center of town. The men followed closely behind, clubs in hand.

I was running now, dragging Pelatt along, as his legs were not as long as mine. I stumbled but caught myself and continued on. A pebble passed my face through the air and flew behind me. We had finally come upon a small gathering of protesters, and one of them had thrown the stone at my pursuers. Another rock flew by, but these did not seem to deter the *asdesaj*. I darted down Iromal Street—the final leg between Pariatt and Kalal— and neared a larger group of my fellows. "*Asdesaj!*" I called out to them. The protesters turned to face us. Had I brought the violence to these people?

But they did not run. They stood their ground. So, when we reached their ranks, I turned to face the *asdesaj* as well. They had stopped at the corner, and were now merely staring at us, clearly, heavily outnumbered. A period of silence ensued, as one pack stared down the other, waiting for them to act. Then, one of the *asdesaj* turned around and began to walk hastily away. They all followed his lead, disappearing out of sight down the street.

Pelatt and I looked at one another, in disbelief of what had just happened. The people around me did the same. And then, all at once, we began to cheer in celebration. We had scared our enemies off. We had defeated them.

I took a few steps down Iromal to continue toward the center of town, but many of those around us began to run in the opposite direction. They seemed to be in pursuit of the fleeing *asdesaj*. "Shall we, as well?" Pelatt asked.

I paused. I wanted to see what would happen, and I was so full of anxious excitement at the pursuit I had just escaped that I felt like showing the *asdesaj* how we would react if they sought our end again, now that we had such great numbers. "No," I said, shaking my head. "I fear they might turn to violence, and I do not want to take part in such actions. Let us continue our peaceful protest, now that our enemies have been fended off."

For the rest of that night we saw no more sign of the *asdesaj*. Perhaps that encounter on Iromal Street had been the final battle for twilight, the last stand for those who used violence and intimidation to control the people. I returned home the following morning full of hope, excited at the victory from the previous night.

With the *asdesaj* in retreat, we were able to focus on other small-scale tactics. We continued to spread news of the *parebhur* and the *evatarr* through word of mouth amongst trusted friends. We learned about an impending raid at the Qholidal School, an academy rumored to have liberal leanings. In times past—the days of the Kalal School, for example—we would have had no choice but to evacuate the academy. But now times had changed, and instead, we devised a manner of resistance. Several dozen of us, perhaps even a hundred protesters, arrived early on the appointed morning, all dressed in the pale green tunics that the Qholidal students wore. There were so many of us that we filled the road entirely, and standing at one corner, it was impossible to see ten feet down the street.

Fifteen *asdesaj* passed by around noon, and came within feet of us. I had not seen this many of them at once in weeks. We braced ourselves, prepared for some sort of action, for them to abruptly take their clubs to those of us in the front of the crowd. But once they caught sight of us and our numbers, they whispered a few words amongst themselves and then continued on down the street.

"When we are willing to act in force together, we take both the day and night," I noted to Pelatt. Once again, I wished that Yhako and Ansidrion had been here to see this. I might have brought down the Kalal School, but I had helped save the Qholidal School. At that moment, it seemed that there was nothing we could not do.

The weather had begun to warm dramatically, and the night after the Qholidal School was saved, Pelatt and I went out onto the streets to find that the snow had melted entirely. "The sun has returned to Ilepya, and I believe we should welcome it by calling for change," Pelatt said, smiling. "I am pleased to do so in such great company."

"Indeed." I nodded. "With the snow gone away from the ground, I should expect we might begin to sweat in such crowds tonight." Something about that moment felt special, and I began to hope that this was the night when we would take our first civic building, or chase a city official from town.

We took our first steps out onto Trafgha Street and I felt comfortable leaving my coat at home. For the third night in a row, Pelatt abandoned his cane, and he walked as if in perfect health. His face, even in its neutral, relaxed form, had grown a handsome, gracious smile and eyes that were full of life, and he nearly walked upright again.

The warm night air had lured many others into the streets early, as well, and before we had even arrived at Turka Street, the roadways were packed full of people. They had begun chanting *"asibavkelumen sakelgareim!*—out with tyrants!" Pelatt and I did not take part in violent chants, as when our fellows occasionally cried "death to the Dictator," but we willingly joined in on peaceful calls for change.

The people seemed emboldened, and we were now moving along Pariatt Street past Turka. "This is as far west as we have gone!" I exclaimed to Pelatt, my voice full of nervous, worried excitement. But as the people before us continued to press ahead, so too did we. Maidia Street, the center of town that we had so longed to go to and so desperately avoided, appeared before us. The people, as if by some magical lure, some undeclared force, were being drawn unto the central plaza!

I glanced at Pelatt as we proceeded, but his face was unreadable. "It appears that we shall go to the Apgha," I whispered to him. "Should we take caution?"

"I am frightened but I am eager," he admitted. I was eager too, but I worried that my fear might shortly get the better of me.

Then, just as Pelatt and I were to turn north onto the fabled Maidia, I heard cries of *"asdesaj!"* The police had shown! I looked out ahead, toward the front of the crowd, and saw the largest swarm of the men in the blue coats I had ever known. We had never encountered such a response before! Was this show of force a retribution for the protection of the Qholidal School?

I could not see what was happening ahead, for there were at least two hundred men and women between the enemy and me. Should we run? Suddenly, I was struck with an idea. We had committed no crime, and how could police use force against law-abiding citizens who did not resist? "We should sit in silence," I suggested to Pelatt. He looked at me and frowned. Of course, the idea did not sound brilliant aloud, especially considering that these protests had begun after a violent raid on innocent timberers. But I was determined to show my cause through peace, and the only way I knew to deal with extreme violence was through extreme peace. "We should do nothing but sit in silence, ignoring them as they approach. Will they kill all of us? There will be no one left in the city for them to exploit!" I doubted I might convince very many of the people around me, but it was worth a try. But as I looked to confirm with Pelatt, I saw him slip away back through the crowd. "Pelatt!" I cried. Where was he going?

I turned to follow him, but with his small frame, he moved easily through the clusters of people. Perhaps he realized that he could not yet run at a good speed, and if we were to escape from the *asdesaj*, he would need quite a lead before them. He soon disappeared from my sight, so merely on conjecture I hastened toward home, abandoning my plan for passive resistance. But as I passed Eparam Street, I instinctively glanced south, toward the old temple. I had not even looked consciously, but I spotted Pelatt, five paces down the street. I took several steps toward him, and then I saw the cane in his hand. How had it come here? He had left it at home. Then, I saw the man crumpled on the ground before him. Pelatt dropped the cane, breathing heavily. "What have you done?" I cried. He did not respond or even look at me, but only stared down upon the broken man at his feet.

This man's coat had become matted with blood, although it had not dried yet. His right leg was twisted behind him. He was still—his breathing, his writhing in pain, had by now ended. I looked at his face and saw that it was bloodied and bruised. It was a horrific sight and I looked away immediately, but it had been enough time for the image to be etched into my mind. I knew the man. Masbat, my old priest, had been beaten to death with his own cane.

We stood there in silence for several minutes, frozen in shock. Then, abruptly, I began to walk toward home, indifferent to the protests and chaos in the streets around me. Pelatt ran after me. "Fe'n, wait!" He called. "Fe'n, I am sorry. I did not intend to do it."

"But you have done it," I whispered, refusing to slow my pace as he struggled to keep up with me. "You have killed a man with your own strength—the strength that you gained from my hospitality."

"But Fe'n! My friend! I did not will it!" He objected. "I saw the man in a side street and lost control of myself. I chased him down and, before I knew it, he lay dead before me."

I turned down Trafgha Street and neared the house, Pelatt still in tow. "When I took you into my home, you insisted that after I could keep you no longer, I should let you go," I reminded him. "That time has come, for I shall not give comfort to a man who does such things by his own hands."

"Where shall I go?" He asked, through tears now. We were standing at my door. "There is no place else for me to stay."

"That is not my concern. You have the clothes on your back, which I have supplied to you in good faith."

"But good Fe'n, I have loved you as a brother should, and although I made a terrible transgression, but please permit me another opportunity at your gracious hospitality."

"You cannot call yourself my brother, for my brothers are Ansidrion the martyr and Yhako the brilliant and heroic philosopher. No man who uses violence shall remain in my home. Now I have given you the strength of two months' care, and the debt I owed unto you for my complicity in your attack has been repaid. Let you go forth, and not come calling at this household again." I turned and began to walk in the door. I knew that I was bound to lose the argument if it carried on much further, for I loved Pelatt deeply and pitied him. But he had done a terrible thing and made a grievous error, and if I were truly devoted to the end of violence, I had to stand firm even against him.

"It is all lost now!" He cried. I had never heard him speak with such despair, and I could hear that his throat had drawn tightly closed in fear and sorrow. Even when he lay on the floor as Ma't had beaten him, even as he cried out in anguish, he had not sounded so despondent. I turned to look upon him once more and I saw that he had collapsed to the ground, his hands desperately rubbing his right thigh. "It has returned! I cannot walk anymore, for without your care my progress has gone away!"

I felt my heart begin to soften. He was a gentle, guileless man, and if he made such a claim, I knew that it was true, for he had no capacity in his entire being to lie. But that gentleness—that nobility in labor that he had once had—was gone now. A truly gentle man, the true Noble Laborer, could not kill another, no matter what that person had done to him. Everything that I had ever known about Pelatt had, in a moment, become untrue. "I wish you well," I told him, and left him collapsed in the alley as I retreated to inside of my home.

III

I slumped into my bed. The night hours drew to a close and the sunlight entered through my open window, but I remained flat on my back. In the moments immediately following my condemnation of Pelatt, another horrifying reality had come over me. I had suddenly felt an awful turning in my stomach and a great weakness in my legs, as though an unbearable burden were suspended from them. I had, naturally, assumed this was all due to my sorrow, to my sickness at what I had witnessed that night. But as the hours wore on it refused to relent, and I found that I could not even move from my bed. The sun's rays crept across the room once again, and after hours of agony and weakness, I found that night had returned. Yet still I had neither strength nor will to move.

The end had come, I told myself. I had been abandoned by all those who loved me. I had met nothing but misery and sorrow, and all of my attempts had been in vain, I scolded myself, dispatching a great despair into my mind. Soon this emotional pain was so strong that it succeeded in drowning out the pains in my body.

If only Yhako and Ansidrion had been here to see this, I had said, just two nights ago. Yes, if only they could see me now. Ansidrion would say that it all—the Ilepyan Brotherhood, the protests—had come to naught, for the *asdesaj* had taken the day, and our family had been left in misery. Yhako had nothing to come back to, for his foolish remaining brother had taken a violent vagrant into the home, and had given away the movement thereby.

But would Yhako even return home? Perhaps he had been killed on the road to Grontinion. Of course he had. The *asdesaj*, the government, the enemies had brought everything to an end. Even Pelatt had been corrupted, his mind filled with violence, such that I had no power to exile it, despite my earnest efforts. There was no more resisting our enemies. I decided that I should just remain in bed, waiting for the *asdesaj* to come to my door, as they surely would following their victory, and deal with me as they had all of the other reformists.

I could see Yhako. Yes, he was there before me! Or, he was somewhere, but I could not be sure where either of us was. I could see the *sinedratha*, the star-shaped symbol of the reform in Grontinion. There were dozens of them, hundreds of them, and they danced about above him in the lavender sky. Yhako smiled and said my name, and I felt comfort for the first time in hours. He was walking hand-in-hand with a beautiful woman, and she said my name as well. I longed to hear it again, for she had the most soothing voice I had ever heard, and I at once felt that I had been waiting many years to hear it. The woman began to make music with her voice, and at some times it sounded like a slow, peaceful song that I had once known many years before. But at other times it was music that I did not understand.

The two pressed on, further and further into the distant sky, until they became specs of dust, and I could no longer perceive them as distinct from anything else. The Grontinion stars, my brother, the beautiful woman and her music were all gone now, and instead I merely saw the room before me, just as I had left it. No, Yhako was here again! I sat up in my bed and he smiled at me. I sighed in a deep relief, elated that he had returned safely. But then I realized that I dreaded to tell him of our failures. There was nothing but disaster to share with him. Worse still, when we faced the greatest threat, I had retreated to my home, and declined to join my fellows in the street. No, I could not face Yhako again. I shut my eyes as tightly as I could, attempting to will him from my presence.

But he approached me and rested his hand firmly upon my shoulder. "Fe'n," he whispered. No, I was too ashamed! "Fe'n, are you well?" He asked. His voice had changed. "Fe'n?"

I opened my eyes and found a strange man standing before me. This was not Yhako. Who invaded my home? No, I knew him! I blinked several times. "Etiar," I said, my voice muffled from having not spoken in a day. The friendly grocer had come. "What brings you here?"

"I came to bring your weekly delivery unto you, sir. When I called out there came no response, so I sought you to ensure your health."

My health? Hum, how did I feel? What had happened? "Ah, I have slumbered this night," I admitted to him. Yhako had come to me in a dream. And then I remembered Pelatt and Ma't. Had that been a dream as well? I looked around the room but saw no sign of the Noble Laborer. "Pelatt!" I called.

But Etiar looked at me, confused. "There is no one I saw within your home."

That part had not been a dream. No, it was too vivid. The memory of the priest's body on the ground burst into my head, and I found that, although I did not witness the attack, I could reimagine the scene in my mind. My stomach twisted in knots.

"Sir, are you well?" Etiar asked.

"No." I was in misery. I was devastated. I had suffered great loss. I thought of all of the horrible things I had seen in the street. I saw people attack one another, canes and clubs and fists being used to great effect. I remembered the *sinedratha* from my dream, and then I remembered that I had once seen it carved into a man's face.

But certainly, I was not as bad off as that man. I still had my body and I still had my home. Yes, I had suffered grief, but that grief was not the deepest of any Ilepyan. And Yhako—there was still the hope that I had in Yhako, bolstered by his safety as I had seen it in my dream. "But I shall be," I amended my response. "I suppose I am merely hungry." Yes, hungry. I had neither eaten nor slept in ten weeks, and although I had not required it before, missing a night of protest meant missing that substitute for my sustenance, so now I needed the real thing.

"Well that much we can treat," the grocer said, smiling, "for here, I have brought you some bread, a few apples, and a great bunch of spinach. Let you eat them now, and all will be well." It was simple enough. I allowed Etiar to feed me, and then, feeling improved, I made my payment as usual.

"Better now?" He asked.

"Yes, better," I acknowledged. "There is still much to do, much to remedy, but I must admit I am better than I had been."

"I am glad for it," Etiar responded. Then he patted my shoulder. "Be well, Federan. If you need anything more, I shall bring it to you."

"Thank you, Etiar. I believe I have everything I need at this moment."

The grocer left the house and I settled back into bed. Things were not as bad as I thought they had been. I would be able to pick up and carry on, even if I did not know what I would do next. The protests had met their end, and the *parebhur* and *evatarr* only brought sorrow into my mind because they reminded me of Pelatt. But there would be something.

Suddenly, I heard voices coming from outside of the house. What was this? Had the *asdesaj* come for us, capitalizing on their victory from the other night? I slowly lifted myself from the bed—some strength had returned, but I was still feeling the great fatigue in my stomach and legs. Then I made my way toward the window. "*Yhahram alu*," I heard a voice cry. "*Peilav kelgarim*," another said. They were reformists!

"*Yhahram alu!*" I cried out into the city. The strength of my voice surprised me. A few others repeated the call in the distance. None of this had made sense. That group of *asdesaj* was so large, so determined, that I was sure they would eradicate us. Instead, here the reformists were, protesting in the middle of the day, and on Trafgha Street. What a turn this had been!

I began toward the door at once, none of the usual caution binding me. I found that I was stronger than I expected, and my legs no longer felt as heavy. But as I ran outside and turned onto the road, I discovered something that was to invigorate me even more. Men and women filled the streets, and it seemed as though the entire population of the city had come here. I heard a few cries and chants, and saw some people running through the crowds, but most people ambled slowly west, speaking casually with the others at their sides. How had this come to be? Was I dreaming again?

"*Yhahram alu*," I called once more, and a few people in my vicinity glanced at me before taking up the call themselves. I heard it spread throughout the street and beyond.

If this was how small, quiet Trafgha Street looked, how would Pariatt, Turka, and Iromal Streets be? I pushed my way through the crowds, turning north onto Malqhom Street, where there were dozens more people. I continued on Pariatt, where the street was wider, and yet it was still full of people, marching west. I followed the crowds, but to my surprise, we passed Turka Street and continued on. We were heading toward Maidia Street! Would the *asdesaj* be there to stop us, just as they had been the other night?

But no, we came to Maidia Street and the crowds only continued north, unabated. We were not merely going to Maidia Street; we were approaching the Apgha itself.

Along Maidia Street, people behaved as they had on the other roads, but there seemed to be a great, smothering feeling of intensity and purpose. They shouted *yhahram alu*, they ducked in and out of alleyways, they ran and they sang. They carried with them a sense of urgency, and when a lovely woman next to me began singing a familiar hymn, I wondered if she was the woman from my dream with Yhako. But then I realized that she could not be. She sang the anthem with the same quick aggression as the other people of the streets. The woman in my dream had sung the song softly and with love; on the streets it sounded like a battle cry.

Finally, the Apgha appeared in sight. Then, I came to an enormous crowd of people, all standing still, facing that building. There were shouts in front, while the people around me whispered and watched. But nothing seemed to be happening from what I could see. The shouting slowly crept toward us, and soon I could make out the words. "Jorda Maqheba," one man said. Then a woman called "Yhari Edlar." There were many people calling out names at once, and I could not hear all of them. What had we come here to do?

After some consideration, I decided that these were names of people who had been killed by the government. Whose name would I say? Of course, Ansidrion was the obvious choice, but what about Sirlat? She had been a martyr of the revolution. She had been partially vindicated by successes in Yafia, yes, but this was her fight too, and she had given her life for it. I wondered how many others around me had more than one name to say.

I prepared to shout out both of my departed siblings' names. Then, suddenly, I heard a familiar voice.

"Yhonam Gavor." Could it be the same Yhonam I had met my first night in the street? Had she been killed as well? I glanced in the direction from which the sound came. There I spotted a woman with the same bright eyes from that autumn night. It was my Yhonam.

I paused a moment and took a breath. Then I said "Federan Ponyhubiresh." I shouted my name as loudly as I could. Let all the crowds hear it, let Yhako hear it, let the Bishop in the Apgha hear it—I had returned to the streets and I would not be intimidated again. We all shouted our guilty names at the oppressors within the Apgha, as a way to say "I am not afraid." At that moment it seemed a more powerful phrase than *yhahram alu*. It captured the same message—a declaration of personal enlightenment by way of the reform. But it did more: it proclaimed to those in power that they could no longer rely on their subjects' fear in order to govern.

Immediately after shouting my name, I began to walk through the crowds, directly toward the Apgha. I had spent enough time in the back, enough time using others to shield me. A few people glared at me, as no one else seemed to be pushing forward. But I was not to be put off. "Let now be the moment that I am part of the action, rather than merely the one who stands back and observes, questions, and records," I said aloud.

It was not until I came to within about ten feet of the gates of the building that I noticed that something different was happening here. These protesters in the front had already grown impatient with uttering their own names, so now they began to press forward. The iron gates were closed firmly against them, so the rebels grabbed hold and shook them wildly. The gates were perhaps a hundred years old or more, and they made a terribly loud, clanging sound when this happened. The people all shouted different words at once, and their many messages were lost in the clamor, and they used their strength against one another. They had demonstrated such discipline only a few minutes ago, but now they had lost it when the time of action came.

"People of Ilepya," I called out to them. "Let you speak one message together! Let you use your force at once, in but one direction!" But the many sounds that they made caused my voice to be inaudible.

We were adrift now, without anyone or anything to lead us. We had become wild creatures, in desperate need of direction. I watched as a man used both the iron rods and the arms and shoulders of the people around him to scramble up over the gates. He seemed to be motioning for others to climb, to follow him over, but none of them did. I could not see him on the other side, and I did not witness what became of him. I could only judge that his idea did not meet positive results, as no one else did as he had done.

Perhaps there were *asdesaj* waiting opposite of that gate. If we crossed one by one, we were doomed to our slaughter. But I knew—as I am sure many of my fellows did—that if we could all enter through the gates at once, we would overwhelm whatever was within. I pushed as close to the gate as I could and heard a hearty-looking man on my left cry "death to the dictators!" A woman on my right was saying "blood finds blood!" No, none of these would do. Then I heard a man chanting *"yhahram alu."* Yes, this was good enough, and what was more, it was easy. I began to chant along with him, being careful that my tone and speed matched his, in order that our voices might best carry. He noticed this and became louder as well. We continued in this way for a minute, with no result.

I did not become frustrated or lose patience. Instead, I altered my tactic. Continuing to chant, I tapped a woman and motioned for her to join in. Then I found a fourth to say it, and she brought with her a few more friends. Now our voices began to dominate the other sounds, and one by one I heard other voices join ours. Soon the chant was one, and I knew that whoever was inside of the Apgha could hear our message, rather than our anger. This was the priority. Then, as our voices became united, so did our force. As if by enchantment, we began to pull at once, concentrating all of our strength. The gate was instantly torn from its hinges. We collectively paused a moment to marvel at what we had done, and then we threw the thing forward, and it fell with such great force that it briefly bounced up again, before landing flat upon the stones behind it.

Now there was a great rush, as people scrambled past one another to enter the Apgha. I considered charging forward with them, but then I conceived of a different plan, and took a few steps within the gate and out of the path. I watched as dozens of men and women flowed in toward the doors. They brought those down easily and then pushed intside of the building. The flow of people continued on and on, and it seemed as if the whole world were entering through the broken-down gate, past the battered doors, and into the Apgha. The people were acting as one body now, and none of them appeared to be in control of his or her motions, but instead each one gave in to the will of the crowd. I felt, at that moment, that this great stream of people would wash the tyranny from Ilepya, bringing ashore a new era of peace and accord. But what other consequences might this great event bring? The people would overthrow the Bishop and his government within, and then there was no predicting what violence, destructon, or even oppression this overwhelming crowd might also achieve in their eager delirium.

For now, I could not be concerned with such things, for I had a different task ahead of me. I am sure it seemed trivial to those around, but to me it was the most important of all. "Let us take down this great fence, as well," I called out. The crowds either did not hear me or did not care. They were focused on the Apgha, the glorious moment within, and perhaps the looting to follow. But I needed these gates gone. I tried to stir a few people toward my cause, as I had done with their chanting, but it was to no avail. No one was willing to halt the wave long enough to listen to the words of a sickly, underfed young stranger.

But then I looked down at my arms. They were stronger than ever. I was underfed, yes, but over the course of two hours, I had ceased to be sickly. How easily I had forgotten! It is the streets that regenerate the people of Ilepya. It is in the roads, speaking against evil and oppression, that good Ilepyans find their rest. What is there more rejuvenating than finding common cause with your neighbors, and speaking out for what is right? Yes, on this day, I had become healthier with every step I took, stronger with every person I encouraged, sharper with every *yhahram alu* I had uttered. How could I doubt my strength?

Suddenly, just as these thoughts wrought their way through my mind, the other gate crashed down before me and crumpled into several pieces. Of course, this was due to a number of factors. The gate was old, and had certainly been loosened by protesters shaking and shoving it. And perhaps the first gate had in some way supported it. There are many reasons which, through science, would explain why the thing would fall down at that moment. But I was beyond them, for I felt that the gate had acted in response to my thoughts. I was so strong that I required minimal real force to achieve my desired goal. It was the power of my will, not my body, which mattered. My will was that the whole of the fence needed to come down in that evening, and I felt that nothing could stop me.

So, as if under some sort of spell, I walked to each segment of the iron fence that isolated the Apgha from the people, laid my hands upon it, and then tore it from the ground using very little of my muscular strength. I continued this until the entire fence surrounding the complex was in pieces on the ground. It was a gargantuan task, and had required perhaps an hour or more, but miraculously I felt no fatigue when it was complete. I know that there is very little reason to any of this. I should have been feeble considering how I had cared for myself over the previous two months. The fence should have required several people to uproot it, just as it had required several to plant it. And such a chore should have left me collapsed on the ground for how much force it took. Yet none of these things were true. I cannot explain the science of it, only to say that I had just experienced one of the many minor marvels of the revolution.

"The government belongs to the people," I said, again to no one. By now everyone had entered the building, returned home, or carried on to their next activity, such that no one was within earshot of me. But I did not say these words for the people to hear them; I said them to make them more true to me. "The government belongs to the people. Its home should be open to them, not fenced off and guarded." And then, giving no time to survey the results of my action, I marched toward the entrance of the Apgha, in order to witness what my fellow revolutionaries had done within.

A few steps inside of the great complex, I realized that the revolution was not as glorious here. There was, as I expected, great destruction inside. The building already looked as though it had not been inhabited for a decade or more, as furnishings were all destroyed and nothing remained in its original condition. What rugs that were still on the floor had been shredded, and a number of words, phrases, and images had been carved into walls and tapestries. The place had been thoroughly looted, and there was no sign of the valuables that had surely once adorned the rooms. "All of this belongs to the people," I reminded myself. It had no business being locked up within this building, as great treasure being controlled by few elites. But if the wealth was any better in the hands of the people who had stolen it, I could not say.

It was dark within, as night had begun to fall and none of the lamps had been lit. Indeed, most of the things that brought or regulated light—lanterns, candles and windows—had been destroyed. It was difficult to see more than a pace ahead of me, but I stumbled through a few corridors and lesser rooms before arriving in what appeared to be a great meeting hall.

There were corpses within. I did not see them, and it was too soon to smell them, but I knew for certain that there had been violence and loss of life wrought here. If not this evening, then it had happened already or was going to happen. The Apgha would not have been left unguarded unless those who occupied it had been killed or had abandoned in fear of their lives. If they had fled, they could not have gone far. Either they were in hiding here in Ilepya, or they were in the reactionary villages of Galmosto or Kapabaj seeking haven.

If any of them remained alive to see what we had done, the message was clear: we have destroyed the building you have used to oppress us, and we shall do the same to you when you return.

I was glad because I did not think the Apgha should be so impenetrable by ordinary citizens. Either the government should rule by its people's consent, or there should be no government at all. I tried not to think of the people who might have lost their lives. Cruel oppressors though they were, they did not deserve such treatment. I wanted the Bishop's government to be eradicated only because of the violence that it inflicted on people. If the

Bishop and his allies would not attack others, I would gladly tolerate their presence and perhaps even their governance. But it could never be so now, as the government and its henchmen had shown themselves to be the permanent aggressor against reformists.

After exploring the dark interior for no more than an hour, I concluded that there was no benefit of my presence in the Apgha. There was no work left to do there. The protesters had all cleared out now, and the palace was empty except for a few dozen otherwise homeless families who had now holed themselves up in different corners, burning furniture scraps for light and warmth. The battle was over and there was nothing left of the field. Remaining here would only further expose me to discoveries of previous violence, and I did not want to take any further of this risk without possible benefit.

I returned to the streets. It was dark now, and to my surprise, there were only a few people out. A pair of men stood conversing in the plaza directly across from me, and I saw about fifteen people walking briskly, some headed in each direction.

In my curiosity, I ran to the men in the plaza. "*Yhahram alu,*" I cried out to them. "Good evening, gentlemen."

I paused briefly to catch my breath. The men seemed surprised at my approach. "*Yhahram alu,*" they hurriedly replied.

"Sirs, why are there no protests? Have they ended?"

"Ended?" The men both spoke at once. Then they chuckled. "No, we walk the streets daily. The protests shall not be over until the Dictator and all of his oppressors are gone from Hihaythea," one of the men insisted.

"Yes, but I mean to say: have they ended for the day? Why is there no one on the streets at this hour?"

They looked at one another and frowned. "Night protest, you mean?" The other man asked. I nodded. "We have won. Did you not see what became of the Apgha?"

"I did, yes. But you said the protests shall not be over. Then why have they stopped?"

"They have not stopped. We shall protest in the day now. We have won here, and there is no reason for cover of darkness when the *asdesaj* no longer own the light."

I felt as though I were in a new society entirely. A whole world had begun anew in the short time since I had last protested. "Then how will we spend our nights now?" I asked. "There is so much more time available for the reformist than ever before!"

"The nights are for each person's own determination. I suppose some might even be sleeping shortly."

"It is a marvel," I said. "It is as though everything has changed in a matter of hours."

"It is true," the second man agreed, smiling. "Everything has changed, and I believe it still must all change again, for something must be built in place of this." He motioned toward the Apgha.

I sighed, amazed by what had happened, and how much we still had yet to do. We had overthrown a government, but we still had to replace it with something, all as the shadow of the national government in Poonlon loomed over us. But there would be time for that later; let now be a time for celebration.

"Tell me, do you live near to here, young friend?" The second man asked.

"I live off of Trafgha Street, perhaps a mile or two to the south."

He looked into the distance for a moment, as though attempting to remember something. Then, he said "our home is on Tajarr Street, not two blocks from the port. Let you come to our home this night, as it is close by, and you may return to your house in the morning."

"Thank you, sirs, but that will not be necessary. I can make my way home just fine."

"I hesitate to think what the streets will be like at night now," the first man argued. "Perhaps they will be safe, perhaps they will be empty. But perhaps, now that most protesters have returned home, our enemies will emerge from their hiding to attack the few who remain. Come, we shall be glad to host you. We would love to share our home with one of our fellows."

"Very well," I responded. "I shall accompany you. And, as I am your guest, it is only right that I share my name. I am Federan, but you may call me Fe'n."

"Come along, Fe'n," the second man said, and we began walking east toward the port. "My name is Abhard Ahibari, and this is my brother Alimarr."

I smiled at once, as I knew who these men were. What was more, when I provided them my family name, I would become familiar to them, although they had never known and perhaps not even heard of me before. Yet another miracle of the revolution, that I would encounter these heroes on this night.

"Gentlemen, it is good to see you alive and well," I said as we hastened toward the coast. "You have known my brother, although perhaps so much has since happened that you have not thought of him in many weeks. His name was Ansidrion Ponyhubiresh, and he toiled with you in the Ilepyan Brotherhood."

Alimarr stared at me in amazement and Abhard clapped his hands together. "Old Ansidrion! That mountain of a man! You must be the boy I met, the young brother Ansidrion spoke so well of." Both men were smiling now.

"Ansidrion was a good man," Alimarr spoke. "Although it has been a while since I thought of him, please know, Fe'n, that Abhard and I never cease to work in the honor of our old fellows. I remember and cherish those twenty-six other members of the Brotherhood, the people who lost their lives that night. We have since spent every one of our nights in the streets, have enforced the *tarbhasht*, the *parebhur,* and the *evatarr*, have and will risk our lives that they have not died in vain."

I smiled meekly. Would that I could say the same, but at least I had been there for the fall of the Apgha. Then I realized something. "Are their lives lost? Perhaps they are locked there in the Apgha!"

"If only it were so," Alimarr said, sighing. "But we were among those who rushed the building when it fell, and we freed the prisoners who were kept within there. But neither Ansidrion nor any of the other members of the Brotherhood were found. It is all but certain, and I am afraid we must accept that they have been killed."

I breathed in deeply and shut my eyes. Yes, I had accepted Ansidrion's death many months before, but this had been the last chance, the last bit of hope. With the Apgha fallen, there was no prospect of his return.

I felt a hand on my back and opened my eyes to Abhard, looking at me with pity. But this was a joyful night, and I imagined how happy Ansidrion would be at what had happened. I did not want to dwell on his loss, for there would be many more hours for that later. "Sirs, we are close to success," I said. "This is thanks in no small part to your hard and brave work."

"Success is at hand, Fe'n." Abhard nodded. "And no single person deserves the praise for it. That praise belongs instead to everyone who has sacrificed anything, including you and your brothers."

I disagreed that I had done much at all, but I decided against saying anything of it. When we arrived at the Ahibari home, Alimarr generously offered me his bed, but I refused it. "I have spent many hours in bed of late,"

I told them. "Tonight I shall accept nothing less than the floor of my gracious hosts."

"Very well, Fe'n, as you will have it," Abhard agreed. "We have a small parlor in the front of our home, and we offer you a few extra blankets to keep you warm through the night."

I thanked the men and followed them into the parlor. I took no time to look around the room, but rather placed my body on the ground, expecting that I might want sleep after such a long day. My hosts departed for their bedchamber, leaving me in the dark with my thoughts.

Of course, the moment I laid myself down, my mind began to race. I had had my night's restoration in the streets, and now I did not need sleep at all. It was not as though I would be able to find it anyway, as I had so much to give my thoughts to. Reform had taken the day. The protesters had been willing to shout their names publicly, at the building that had represented their oppression. And that very building, the Apgha, had fallen to the people. It was all a marvel to me. Had we already been this close to success when I retreated to my bed, or had it all come about in one day?

I began to think of Yhako and Ansidrion, of Pelatt and Ma't, and all of the many people who might have different thoughts about the events of this day. Soon I found myself sitting upright upon the floor, and then, as the weak light of dawn began to creep in through the window, I took a brief stock of the room. It was nothing of particular remarks, and had I not looked to the shelf over the small stove, I would certainly give no word of anything therein. But in the spring early morning light, I could see that the brothers had a few small books resting upon this shelf. I was feeling both curious and restless, naturally, so I stood and looked through them.

The cover of the first book, to my great surprise, bore the words *asdelma Galmostaya*—the Song of Galmosto. I knew this book, of course. I had read it many times in my youth, had placed great faith in it for my first eighteen years, and had since given it great criticism. This was a prayer book, which had been denounced by the reform. What was it doing in the home of two honored opposition leaders?

I looked to the next book. Perhaps they merely owned it to better understand their opponents. But all of the books were similar—books praising the Lords' Occult and the Iqharepur, books that no one in Grontinion held in any esteem. Might the Ahibaris follow the old religion? Had they lured me into their home to do me harm? Had they been spies within the Ilepyan Brotherhood all along? Or did they merely have the books as research of their opponents, or as relics of a past life?

My mind had been filled with questions, with contradictory explanations. At that moment, however, I heard a great commotion from outside of the house and footsteps just beyond the door. I rushed to the small window in the room to see men and women running eastward. What could this be? An attack? But after a moment of observation, I noticed in the dim light that the people smiled and waved their companions along. They were running toward something. I made my way to the entry of the house, where I saw my hosts standing in the doorway. Just as I arrived, a man addressed the brothers as he ran by. "Abhard, have you heard? The Yiffens arrive by sea! Their ships are come to port even now!" The man summoned us with his right hand, and then disappeared beyond the door in the direction of the port.

"We must go!" I cried suddenly. Abhard and Alimarr whirled around to me in surprise. "Apologies, sirs, but I heard the great activity and what that man has said. We must go to the port to greet them!"

Abhard closed his eyes and sighed slowly. Yet another moment we had so long awaited had come. "I must grab my coat and don my shoes," he said. He and his brother both began toward their chamber.

But I could not wait. "I shall see you at the port, for I must go now! Thank you, sirs, for putting me up this night!" I was already out the door, sprinting to the sea. If I felt any guilt at leaving them so abruptly, I quickly forgot of it, as I did the books about Galmosto. Everything was changing so fast that there was no time to dwell even on things that had occurred but moments before.

"Yhako might be on one of those ships!" I said to myself as I ran. I wanted to temper my expectations, to remind myself that he had gone to Grontinion and this support had likely come from Rakka. But my heart leapt merely at the possibility. What if he were here, prepared to set his feet on the soil of Ilepya for the first time in several months? The thought was too wonderful to obsess over, yet also too wonderful to ignore.

I arrived at the port among a crowd of perhaps a hundred others. The women wiped their faces with cloths and the men did off their hats, but all of us in attendance cheered and laughed at our great fortune. However, I could only tolerate so much of this. From where we stood I saw nothing but the crowds of people before me. So I rounded the east side of the harbor, where the land sloped suddenly downward toward the sea. From the east, I could stand at the level of the sea, albeit at a considerable distance from the disembarking ships. I would not be able to welcome the Yiffens as they made landfall, but at least I could see them the moment the disembarked.

I knew my way around the port because, like many Ilepyans, I had been here before. It was here, next to the trading boat slips on the east side, that people carved the names of victims of the Bishop and the *asdesaj* directly into the pier. This, of course, is where Yhako and

I had gone to write Ansidrion's name several months earlier. And now, although there were many more names that approached the base of the wooden pier, the *asdesaj* had not destroyed it, as Yhako had predicted. Perhaps they had not wanted to acknowledge how the pier had been used. It might even have been possible that they were not aware of it.

I crawled slowly toward the front of the pier. I wanted to welcome the Yiffens with Ansidrion. I smiled and ran my fingers along the name of my deceased brother, remembering Yhako's tears as he scratched the letters with his carving knife.

One by one, the Yiffens disembarked from the ships. I began to worry that I would not recognize Yhako from my place. I could not see much more than the shape and gait of the people off-boarding. I stood up to gain a better view, keeping the toe of my shoe upon Ansidrion's name. Just as I stood, I saw a man and a woman, walking hand-in-hand off of the ship and down upon the port. I knew this sight well. I could almost hear the women singing the song from my dream. The man, tall and slender, walking slowly with his chin held high, was clearly Yhako. I had no idea who the woman could be, but it did not matter. My brother was here.

I ran with all of my strength toward the street. I should have been in no hurry; Yhako was here to stay, so why not slow to a stroll? But I was full of energy and excitement, and kept on running, allowing my motive and purpose to outweigh my body's limitations. I approached the port but could not see him. Then, knowing I might find him nowhere else, I turned for home.

When I finally entered the house, I was greeted with a gasp of alarm. The woman was on the ground floor of the house, which had been torn apart. Had she done this? No, she seemed to be just as upset about it as I. Perhaps it had happened the night before, when I was out and the streets had been governed by lawlessness. But there would be time to seek that answer later, for this woman was of far more pressing importance. It was clear that she did not recognize me, and so must have believed that I was an invader to her home. I walked toward her but she backed away. "Qhema," I whispered.

I continued toward her, but she abruptly stopped moving. Surprise gripped her face, as she allowed her jaw to fall aslack and she furrowed her brow.

"Qhema," I said again, smiling this time. "It is me. Do you remember me?"

"Yhako," she cried out, her face having not shaken its look of shock. "Yhako," she shouted again.

"Yes?" I heard my brother's voice call from above and I felt weak with happiness, in disbelief that this moment had finally come.

"You had better come down the stairs, for there is someone here you must see." Still no change in her face. Did she know? I took one more step in her direction, and then she finally smiled broadly. "Federan! Oh Federan, it is you at last!" She stretched her arms out and I fell into them, enjoying her warm, loving embrace. "Oh, Federan, you are a man!" She said, releasing me and looking upon my face.

I nodded. "And you are just as welcoming as I remember, your voice as comforting as always." She had, miraculously, scarcely changed at all, at least in her appearance. I marveled at my failure to recognize her in my dream or, rather, my premonition. She was a bit thinner now, and her skin had grown darker, but her face looked as if it had scarcely aged. She still wore her headdress and her colorful gowns, but they had changed with fashion, and now they were more subdued and no longer flowed gracefully with her movements. She did not wear silk, I noticed, but she probably did not have the access to it that she once did.

I had no time to ask Qhema her fare or what had brought her from Vend, for before I realized what was happening, I had been wrapped up in another pair of arms. Yhako. I embraced him in return, and when he pulled away to look at my face, just as Qhema had, I noticed that I had begun to cry. Tears were streaming from my eyes. Yhako, my greatest ally, my biggest champion, my oldest friend, my brother had returned, safe and healthy. I had never felt as empowered in my life as I had during the previous twenty-four hours, and yet I felt that I had never needed Yhako more than at this very moment.

"Fe'n, you are alive," he said.

There were so many things I had wanted to say just then. Yet all I could muster was "and so are you."

"We had worried for your life when we came to find so many of our things destroyed, and saw that you were not in here," Yhako explained. "What if you had been kidnapped and killed by the *asdesaf*? But here you are, alive and well!"

Yes, indeed, but it was lucky that he had not seen me but one day before, when I was ill and confined to my bed. In that circumstance I would have carried great shame, for I would have been in the depths of my inaction. Now, I had cause to be proud, even if I had rectified it only through a day's labor. "I am so happy to see you alive!" I said. "I did not hear from you for months, and I feared that you had been the victim of an assassin."

"Did you not receive our letters?" He asked, frowning.

"I received one: the Karliott Prophecy. There has been nothing since then."

"Oh Fe'n, I am sorry for that," he said. "I wrote you a letter at every turn, but it is reasonable to expect

GUILTY NAMES

that my messengers could find no safe way to deliver them to you."

"It is of no consequence, for you are here now," I told him. Then I looked at Qhema. "But the two of you must explain everything that has happened since: how you have united, what success you met in Yafia, and who has accompanied your arrival."

Yhako and Qhema glanced at one another. "Very well, I suppose I can tell my part of it," Yhako agreed. "But if I should forget something, beloved sister, please interrupt." Qhema nodded, so Yhako began. "I left Rakka promptly, just as I told you in my letter. I travelled the road to Grontinion alone, as I desired to use the time to reflect upon our struggle and the words Karliott had said to me.

"I finally arrived at Grontinion after eight days of travel. The city is smaller than our Ilepya, yet even so, I was in awe. It was the most beautiful place I had ever visited, and as soon as I passed through the gates, I sensed that I was in a place of great wonder and joy. It was a cold winter's evening when I arrived, yet the city buzzed with spirit, and people filled the streets. I initially feared that I might meet difficulty in finding the University, but all one must do is take a few steps into the streets to realize that the whole town is structured around the great institution. I knew at once that the roads would all lead me there. I am sure this is exactly how you felt when you first came to Grontinion, is it not?" He asked Qhema.

"Oh yes," she confirmed. "One cannot be in Grontinion without instantly realizing where the University is, and it is nearly impossible to walk casually through the streets without happening upon it."

"I wanted to take some time to visit the places that Sirlat had told me about," Yhako continued. "There was the old Vodi Temple, or the beautiful Liziatun Square. But the lure, and the urgency, of the University was irresistible. I made directly for the fabled campus, where a friendly student brought me to a professor, who brought me directly to the great Chancellor Stahrik. I expected them all to greet me with respect when I told them my name, but I was surprised at the ease of access I had to the Chancellor."

"Sirlat's name carries great weight," I suggested.

"It does, but I do not believe that is the whole of it. For as soon as I was introduced to the Stahrik, he shook my hand and said 'I am glad that you are here, for by some great miracle, I have someone whom you must meet.' I was baffled, but the man disappeared from my presence, and returned several minutes later with this amazing woman," he said, smiling at Qhema. "I did not recognize her!"

"I knew him at once," Qhema boasted. "'Yhako,' I cried. 'You have come! How are you here, in the city of Sirlat?' I asked him."

"And for an hour or more we spoke, telling what had become of our lives in the last fifteen years. And then Stahrik told us that he would rouse a small contingent of student volunteers, and give us funds to pay a ship to take us back to Ilepya. It was a bit of a failure on my part, as I had gone to raise an army, but having found Qhema, I wanted nothing more than to bring her back to Ilepya with me. If Stahrik offered us his blessing along with a few dozen lightly-armed volunteers, it was excuse enough for me to end my mission."

"And might I hear Qhema's story?" I asked. "Please, Qhema, tell me what you have told Yhako. How had you gone from your work as a missionary in Vend to a guest of Chancellor Stahrik?" I asked.

"Oh no, Federan," Qhema replied, her face forging into a frown. "I did not serve as a missionary in Vend. This is the last thing I would want you to think I had spent so many years doing. I did go as a missionary, but it was never my intention to spread any religion. I went because the church gave me the opportunity to do something interesting and new, but even before I arrived, I realized that I felt no calling to compel others to believe in a new faith. I came to a large village—Hergus—and simply began to live among the locals.

"As a young, healthy woman, I was capable of labor, but there was always someone who was stronger or more experienced, so I was of little use. I could not earn my keep, and merely had to rely on the charity of the people there to survive. I spent a few nights on the street and had to beg for some of my meals, which was quite a dramatic change for a woman like me, who had been raised in luxury.

"One night, a blacksmith allowed me to come into his family home. Once inside, I gathered my paper and ink—among the few possessions I did not barter away—and began to write an account of recent events, as I often did. The smith was amazed with these actions, and he demanded to know what it was that I did. I explained to him that I was writing as a means of communication, and he marveled that people might communicate with one another despite living many miles apart. He insisted that I teach him to write, as he had a brother far away in another village whom he wanted to send word to. I advised him that his brother would have to learn to read, and he told me 'I shall write him a letter, and you will go unto him and teach him to read it.'

"Of course, this process was illogical if only one letter was to be exchanged, but I thought about all of the joy and light that reading and writing brought me, and how much I could provide this man if he learned to read. 'Very well,' I told him, 'I shall teach you and your brother to read, but only if you will share this knowledge with your sons and daughters, and your neighbors if you are able.' The man agreed, and so, ever slowly, literacy crept into Hergus, which had never known it before.

"I visited the brother, who lived in Vernun, a day's travel away, and spent two weeks with him, teaching him letters. After he had begun to understand the idea, he wrote a response to Hergus, which I duly brought. When I returned I found that many families had taken interest in this new concept, and people were offering to take me into their homes if I would show them this new form of communication."

"'It is a marvel to read and write,' a protester told me in the streets," I remarked. "What a noble thing, to teach others to do so."

"Indeed, I have known only a few pleasures greater than it," Qhema agreed. "I had very little paper, and once it was exhausted, villagers began carving words into stone or whatever other canvas they could find. Then a tanner found himself with a surplus of skins, and recommended that they might be used instead for writing letters. The new product quickly became so profitable that he abandoned tanning entirely, and began to experiment with producing hide more hospitable for ink. Meanwhile, I fantasized about opening a grammar school and teaching everyone in Hergus to read."

"And did you? Is there a Ponyhubiresh School in Hergus today?" I asked.

"Sadly there is not. After I had been in the town for a few years, word reached the bishop and magistrates that new ideas were beginning to spread amongst the populace. A young Hihaythean woman, rumored to be a heretic, had come to the town and taught the laborers to read, and now some of the laborers had even gotten their hands on books. They had read about the revolution in Colof, and were telling their neighbors about these and other dangerous ideas. The girl from Ilepya had to be stopped in order to shelter the locals."

"Yes, I suppose those in power cannot have been very happy that so many people had expanded their potential for knowledge," I proposed. "An illiterate population is easier to control, for they have little to believe other than what those in power tell them."

"That is true, and the authorities knew it. There is no *asdesaj* in Hergus, as there is in Ilepya—the town is not organized enough—but you can imagine they sent whatever brutes they had after me. I fled Hergus and stayed with the smith's brother in Vernun for a time, teaching his neighbors to read. But I knew that I could not remain here long, for it was too close to the capital, in Vend. The closer I came to the central government, the easier they could find and dispose of me. So I fled upriver, into the herding villages in the hills. But, to my surprise and delight, even the people here had heard about the growing literacy, and when they learned that I could read and write, they all hailed me. Families offered me anything they could provide—food, clothing, shelter, and even a few potential husbands—if I would just teach them for a day. I gladly accepted many of their offers, although the suitors I declined."

"It sounds as though you gave them liberty," I said, "for the townsfolk in Hergus were liberated from ignorance, and empowered by their new access to knowledge." Qhema nodded. "Liberty in exchange for their charity, their generosity," I added.

"Hum," Yhako said. Qhema glanced at him. "I have not thought of those ideas since Ansidrion's death, but I suppose they fit," he agreed.

"So what happened next?" I urged Qhema forward. "If the shepherds in the new villages had heard of your work, then surely the government would have received word of you."

"Indeed they did. I knew that I could not remain in any place for very long. I spent many years moving from village to village, going as far east as Omil, and even returning on occasion to Hergus or Vernun. Sometimes I would adopt accents or false names to hide myself, but most people welcomed me, and so I usually could go without concealing my identity. I was not the greatest enemy of the government in Vend, of course, but you would be surprised at how often I was told I had to leave a village because someone had come there from the capital recently, inquiring of my location. There are few things more dangerous to an oppressor than a well-educated woman."

"How long did you live as a fugitive?" I asked.

"Over a decade. But it is not as terrible as it sounds, for I loved the work I did, and I enjoyed being pursued. It is, in some ways, an honor to have a tyrannical government want to eliminate you."

"I suppose the protesters in the streets of Ilepya know that feeling, although no one has wanted me by name. Perhaps that is why we shouted our names at the Apgha, to invite such an honor."

"Shouted your names at the Apgha?" Qhema asked. "Do explain."

"Ah, I apologize, for my thoughts have escaped my head. I shall recount it later, but for now please continue. When did you finally decide to end your time in Vend? How did you find yourself in Grontinion?"

"It was all merely by accident, for I never set about to leave Vend. Several months ago, I wandered deep into the northern hills, near the border with Yafia. I came to a small hamlet, but I found that all of the people there had already learned to read. The residents still welcomed me, but I did not want to be put off from my mission, so the following morning, I moved to the next community. Here, as well, everyone knew their letters, as they did in the next two villages I visited. I did not know where to turn. Surely, my chore was not complete, but I suddenly felt directionless. Then, from atop a hill, I looked over into Yafia and noticed a small village. I realized that perhaps there were Yiffens, too, who might be taught to read. They lived in much greater freedom, of course, but it would be better to teach them than to wander uselessly among fully literate Vendi villages.

"So I set out for Yafia, and found at the first village that many of the locals did not know how to read. But others did, so reading was not novel there. Those who were illiterate had no interest in learning. I considered returning to Vend, but I realized that I was not too far from Grontinion. I had heard that Sirlat had died some years earlier, but I still wanted to see the city, and perhaps speak with some of her friends."

"I did not know Sirlat at all, but I forget that you cannot have known her very well, either," I interrupted. "How old were you when she left? Ten years?"

"I was ten, yes, but I had visited her twice in Grontinion, so the way north from Vend was not entirely unknown to me. Fortunately, although the Yiffens were not interested in learning to read from me, they were still willing to take me in, and I am glad to say that I never spent a night in that country without a roof over my head.

"I arrived at Grontinion after some ten days of travel. I made directly for the University, and Chancellor Stahrik himself took me in. I intended to return to Vend, and had made plans to leave, but Yhako arrived on what I intended to be my final night. I was overjoyed at seeing him, and I was easily persuaded to return to Ilepya. 'Federan is a strong, thoughtful young man, and you will be proud of him,' Yhako told me. I knew at once that I needed to come here."

I looked around the room. In this place of chaos, where so much lay destroyed, I felt safer and more comforted than ever. I had despaired of Yhako's life and had resigned to never see Qhema again. Now here they were both, and I had a family. I could live in this shattered house with them forever.

"I am sure that both of you faced incredible challenges and fascinating trials in your time away from home. I wish I could hear them all now, although I know it would take an eternity to recount all of them."

"I shall tell you them over time," Qhema agreed. "But come, let us hear of your experiences. Yhako has given me some word of how you have become quite the little heretic, in defiance of Mother's will. But what has happened this past winter? We would both like to know."

"Yes, but first let us take a meal together," Yhako said, "for I have not had good Hihaythean food in many weeks."

"I do not have much of that here," I said, "but the good grocer delivered some food yesterday, and we can enjoy what little we have. And if the looters have not gotten to it, I suppose we have some bitter root tea for you, Yhako."

So I told the two of them about the growing protests, my return to the streets, my time with Pelatt, and the fall of the Apgha. I left out Ma't's murder and the many days I spent in bed. Yhako and Qhema would hear about these things in time, but I was not ready to recount them yet. Then, after we finished our meal, Yhako and I decided to spend the afternoon walking along Maidia Street, as we had many years before, with Ansidrion. We invited Qhema to join us, but she declined in favor of a nap, perhaps astutely recognizing that Yhako and I needed some time with just the two of us.

We set out, first merely exchanging our fare further, and I shared with him more details about the last several months. There were small groups of people protesting on the streets that day, but otherwise it appeared as though life had returned to normal, although we now felt freer in our speech. When we passed Eparam

Street, I decided to tell him about the murder of the old priest. Yhako offered his condolences for what I had witnessed, and quickly changed the subject, as we continued toward Maidia Square. When we finally approached the Apgha, we fell silent. Yhako studied the fallen gate, the broken windows, and the tattered standards. He said nothing, but merely sighed at the magnitude of it.

"Life certainly has changed in the months since you left," I said at length.

"It has," he whispered. Then I saw a satisfied smile cross his face. "And you have done this, Federan."

"No," I argued back quickly. "I have not done this at all. In truth, Yhako, while brave Ilepyans took to the streets, I was in my bed. I failed to sacrifice as Ansidrion had."

"If we all gave Ansidrion's sacrifice there would be no one left to enjoy the fruits of it. But you have worked for this. You spent many nights in the street, and each one of those nights was a risk on your life. Federan, you are as much a revolutionary as any one of the others."

I thought about my first protest, and the nights with Pelatt in the streets. I had passed many hours in my bed, yes, cravenly hoping others would carry out the revolution on my behalf. But I had also protested, I had also taken part in the *parebhur*, I had shouted my guilty name at the Apgha, and I had helped tear down those awful gates. I was not the single hero, the leading revolutionary I had once fancied myself. But I was one of many who had done his part to bring about profound change. I smiled. "Yes, Yhako, I suppose you are correct. I have done this. And so have you."

"No, I am but a stuffy old academic, kept in his study when the revolution began, fled abroad as it ended."

"Yhako, do not decline this praise, for you have done many things in your own manner. You have risked your life and livelihood to seek help in Grontinion, you have trained and supported your brothers in their activity. You must take your own credit for it."

But Yhako merely shrugged, unconvinced.

"No single person brings about a revolution, Yhako," I continued. "No one deed wins a war. It requires many individual and collective actions by thousands of people. I have been one of those, Ansidrion has been one of those, and you have been one of those. We are no greater than the grocer who simply complies with the *parebhur* and the *evatarr*, but otherwise goes about his daily life. But we are no less than the martyrs who have given everything. Everyone has a part to play, and we all must take pride therein."

Again, Yhako said nothing, but where before he had appeared full of doubts, now he seemed lost in thought. There was no way for me to know what he was thinking just then—pressing Yhako never yielded much result—but for now I contented myself that he was at least considering my argument.

After a few minutes' silence, Yhako placed his hand on my shoulder to indicate he was ready to continue walking. We ambled forward, away from that terrible form, that symbol of crushing oppression that had, itself, been crushed.

"Now that this is done with, what of your Noble Laborer, your Pelatt?" Yhako asked.

I sighed at hearing his name aloud, but to my surprise, I felt no anger at him. My lasting vision of him— or, that is, the one that came to mind first—was not of Pelatt standing over Ma't's battered body, but the sad man, crippled in the street, begging my forgiveness. I did not like his crime; I could never excuse it. But the battle was over. With the dust settled, how many Ilepyans would find blood on their hands? I would have to forgive all of them as well to go on living in this city, because they were my brothers and sisters. In fact, I began to feel as though I already had. Making amends with a former criminal did not excuse his crimes any more than making friends with a former enemy justified his hatred. Perhaps Pelatt had not been the man I thought he was, but that was no more his doing than mine. I had ascribed qualities to him, equated him with a fable, and refused to see him as a human being, capable of flaws.

"Pelatt was not the Noble Laborer, but he was a special man whom I loved and took into my home. He is alienated from me now, but were our paths to cross again, I would treat him to a new shirt and give him a meal, just as I would any other Ilepyan in need."

"He is just another Ilepyan to you now? You no longer hold him above all others?"

"Remarkably gullible and naïve, yet infinitely stubborn; good in nature yet volatile under pressure; charitable, gracious, and gentle, yet flighty and fickle—the Noble Laborer is the Hihaythean people. These are all characteristics of my Pelatt, and they are characteristics of Hihaythea. Therefore, the Noble Laborer is in everyone, and we must look for him in everyone we meet."

Yhako smiled and shook his head. "If that young priest's boy could hear you now, think what he would say."

I smiled. "Yes, I suppose I have changed quite a bit from the narrow-minded child I once was. I have learned more of the ways of the world, and despite all of the hatred, all of the harm there is, I have come to believe most of all in liberty, charity, and generosity."

"I believe we have all seen the benefits thereof in recent times," Yhako agreed.